the
Complete Tales
of
Ketzia Gold

the
Complete Tales
of
Ketzia Gold

a novel by
Kate Bernheimer

Tuscaloosa

Published by FC2 with support provided by Florida State University, the Unit for Contemporary Literature of the Department of English at Illinois State University, the Program for Writers of the Department of English of the University of Illinois at Chicago, the Illinois Arts Council, and the Florida Arts Council of the Florida Division of Cultural Affairs

Address all inquiries to: Fiction Collective Two, Florida State University, c/o English Department, Tallahassee, FL 32306-1580

ISBN: Paper, 1-57366-096-5

Library of Congress Cataloging-in-Publication Data
Bernheimer, Kate.
  The complete tales of Ketzia Gold / Kate Bernheimer.-- 1st ed.
    p. cm.
  ISBN 1-57366-096-5
  1. Young women--Fiction. 2. Fairy tales--Adaptations.
  I. Title.
  PS3602.E76 C66 2001
  813'.54--dc21
                                        2001001127

Cover Design: Todd Michael Bushman
Book Design: Tamika Tatum and Tara Reeser

Produced and printed in the United States of America
Printed on recycled paper with soy ink

The author wishes to acknowledge the German, Russian and Yiddish stories on which portions of this novel are based.

The original tales are:

From the German: "The Ditmarsh Tale of Lies," "The Star Talers," "A Riddling Tale," "Clever Else," "The Girl from Brakel," "Choosing a Bride," "The Girl without Hands," "The Odds and Ends," "The Fox and the Geese," "The Rosebud," "Frederick and Liza-Kate" (*Grimms' Tales for Young and Old: The Complete Stories*, Anchor Books 1977).

From the Russian: "Three Anecdotes," "The Armless Maiden," "Danilo the Luckless," "The Stubborn Wife," "The Beggar's Plan," "The Bad Wife" (*Russian Fairy Tales*, Pantheon 1945).

From the Yiddish: "The Passover Elf Helps Great-Grandmother," "Clever Kashinke and Foolish Bashinke," "Sore-Khane at the Tip of the Church Tower," "The Penitent and the Rebbe of Tshekhenove," "Some True Miracles of God," "The Poor Rabbi and His Three Daughters," "A Topsy-Turvy Tale" (*Yiddish Folktales*, Pantheon 1988).

Four stories also appear transcribed in their entirety from *Grimms' Tales for Young and Old* by Jakob and Wilhelm Grimm, translated by Ralph Manheim, copyright © 1977 by Ralph Manheim: "The Ditmarsh Tale of Lies," "The Star Talers," "The Fox and the Geese," and "The Rosebud." Used by permission of Doubleday, a division of Random House, Inc.

Grateful acknowledgment is made for the generous support of the George Bennett Fellowship in Creative Writing at Phillips Exeter Academy, and to the Arts and Humanities Council of Tulsa, Oklahoma.

Enormous gratitude to R.M. Berry and Brent Hendricks.

And when the needle finally swung
It was wrapped in rags, in pitch blackness.
I escaped from a dream of living
Into a fairy tale with no happy ending, no ending at all.

—John Ashbery

chapter one

The Saltmarsh Tale of Lies

I want to tell you something, so listen. I saw two bathers flying. They flew with their breasts turned heavenward and their backs faced hellward. The first wore a striped bikini, the second a plain pair of trunks. Once I saw a bird in a shake at the boardwalk's fancy ice-cream stand, and then an anchor and some dune grass swam across the bay just as gracefully as you please. The anchor was surprising but dune grass is more lovely. Four girls in eyeglasses tried to catch a rabbit that lived in the mansion lawn. The first girl was sad, the second girl was afraid, the third girl was insecure and the fourth girl was just plain mean. Do you want to know what happened? The first saw the animal and tearfully told the second, who ran away to tell the third, who tried in vain to catch the rabbit. Shut up if you don't believe me. This is all in the country by the sea where a lobster chased me to a field of windflowers enclosed by a wall. Inside I saw a cow, who had gotten there by leaping. There are greenflies and blackflies and dragonflies there. So open the window and let the lies out, I say.

chapter two

Brown paneling and a low ceiling trapped darkness here. The bedroom's only window faced a dead-end street, lined with oaks and maples. The Golds had filled this unremarkable nursery with several fine items for their young girls: the wood rocker with scratchy red upholstery; the white crib painted with dancing elephants and monkeys; and the stiff fur plaything, a seal on wheels, larger than Ketzia at this age, that sat in the middle of the room, waiting to carry her through toddling days. It presided over a kidney-shaped brown shag rug.

Meredith—or, as the family called her, Merry—Ketzia's older sister, lay on her back on a small cot next to the crib. Above Merry's bed hung a monkey, suspended from the ceiling by a spring attached to its head. The monkey sprung toward the ceiling and down again as Merry kicked the bottom of its feet with the bottom of her own. "Monkee-kee, Monkee-kee," Merry said. "My Monkee." It had a rather sickly smile, giant ears and denim jeans.

Ketzia lay in the crib on her stomach, arms twisted, hands palm-down by her sides. Pressing a cheek into the pale pink blanket that would later

be known as "Sniffy" due to an unfortunate "accident" with Mrs Gold's bottle of expensive perfume,
Ketzia launched two green eyes about the room,
noted the orange sheer curtains and the light coming through them—tossing shadows of suburban
leaves on the wall—and perhaps, though we can't
be certain, the stolid gaze of her sister Merry who
looked away at once upon meeting Ketzia's eyes.

chapter three

The Star Pennies

I'm going to tell you something. For a long time I was so poor that I only had one room to live in with a small cot to sleep on. This room was on the road of oracles. You could hear the cars go by through the thin motel door. I did have some real things in storage at my parents' house—a brass bed, an automatic drip coffee maker, a woolen pea coat—but I was too old to go home. And my husband and I were no longer together.

I was tired a lot of the time. I was in a warm place that on the map was always orange, sometimes lined in red. This is on the television, and in the paper. I spent my days walking the desert under the hot sun in a cowboy hat Adam had bought me downtown in another state. We saw the swans that day, and a pigeon ate peanuts off Adam's shoulder while I screeched with fake terror, nearby.

I managed to keep myself fed. I was too proud to ask Adam for money. Money should not pass hands that way, though one must give it to strangers. My parents had lent me so much over the years I was finally too embarrassed to ask them for more. I had learned my lesson well.

I walked down a hot, six-laned speedway every blazing morning to a shop where two teenage boys gave me a plastic bag full of bagels. They did not sell all the bagels every day, they said. "We have yesterday's bagels for you," they said. The boys wore shirts of many colors with bursts of white naked fabric throughout the colors.

Pumpernickel, garlic, sesame, raisin, a wondrous kind called *everything*.

I'd walk west on the speedway, past the road of oracles to a red-rocked hilly place called the monument. Then I wandered up and down dried-out riverbeds. Thorny plants were all about and when the sun set and snakes came out onto the thin-shaded sand, I'd walk east to the road of oracles and leave the desert behind.

Back at the motel I would pass by the office and lower my chin in a kind of greeting. I entered my small motel room through a door that was never locked and felt as though made of cardboard. The manager had given me a cheap monthly rate. He knew I got my money selling plasma. He mostly let rooms by the hour and had a place for me.

As part payment the manager could see me through a glass window that was shady and grey, though I could only see myself. Inside, everything was dark and seemed like a photograph negative.

Each evening I would strip and wash my body head to foot with soap the manager, with his biker's t-shirt and beautiful hair, left on the sink for me daily. This soap was wrapped in white paper and you could smell the soap through the paper when you entered the room from the road. I would hang my brown dress—so delicately flecked with tiny pink roses—in the bathroom, so the steam could straighten all the small wrinkles. I'd pull my hair back into a tight, wet ponytail and face the mirror, dimming my expression and shrinking into my body. Then, I would lie on the bed in my pale slip and let hot tears burn lines on my cheeks. But only for a moment.

Taking a deep breath, I would try to imagine an erotic scene that might save me. I'd stretch my body out so my hands brushed the pressboard wall and my feet dangled in the hot desert air. Lying flat, I would wait for someone to come. I barely slept that entire year, there was so much to hear inside my head, and out. Inside was the waiting game. Outside, coyotes sang. At first I thought I was hearing a gang of weeping children come to cover the earth. Soon their howls sent words and I knew what they meant.

I started to call Adam from the motel desk every morning to tell him. I knew we would not be together, which made me ashamed, so I'd hang up as soon as I heard his voice. Every day I did this, but by winter's end, that first season of no food or money and only me to walk and weep, I was so weak the telephone seemed too heavy for my hand. Yet still I would call. I'd go into the office where the manager would hand me the phone without a word, his head tilted back, mid-dream. I would dial the number and let the receiver thud down to the counter, then leave for my walk. I guess the manager hung it up later, upon waking.

In spring I called for the very last time. I was so hopeless I had decided the whole world had forsaken me and it was only a matter of time until the real end. An owl with a snake in its mouth had flown by my face one dawn, darkening my skin. Telling Adam of my troubles was beside the point, now the true end was on its way.

I continued to walk the desert floor daily. With my stale bagels and in my floral dress and western hat, which I kept quite clean despite my despair, I made a pretty picture for many gaping tourists. "A native," I would occasionally hear one whisper. This struck me as hysterical, for it's all a terrible mistake. Still, I knew much about the desert and I tried to communicate all I knew with my eyes. The end is coming, my eyebrows warned them, heed the prickly pear. If the prickly pear has bloomed, find cover!

One pale day I walked farther than ever. It was the hottest time I had ever known in the desert. Even my bones felt the sun. Everything was dead, dried up in the vast oven of sky and earth. I came upon a man poorer than even myself. "I'm so hungry," he said. His skin looked made of wood. I let the plastic bag fall from my hand and watched as it landed and melted onto a rock. My head burned so, the burning felt cold, and I felt a solitary ice cube melt through my skull. I walked from the man and my bagels.

Soon I found a child resting near a spiny ocotillo. "My head is so cold," the child said. "Mine too," I answered. "My head is so hot, it's cold." She just stared. I took the leather hat Adam had given me and placed it on the child's head. She reached her hands up and felt along its band, patterned with colors and made of bird's feathers. The child leaned against the ocotillo. "No!" I cried, because the ocotillo is like nails. She fell asleep, apparently unharmed. I bid farewell to the hat and the girl.

Farther along, I saw another child. He had no shirt and small circles under his eyes. "Take my dress," I told him. "It's made of rayon, a fabric they say is fine as silk. You can wash it when the monsoons come just by standing beneath a cloud." The dress swept the desert floor as the boy walked away, the dress covered his hands with its long flowing sleeves.

At last I came to the deep saguaro forest, with its angular cacti, tired and old. The sun no longer slapped my head. It was so dark that when the last child asked me for my underslip I thought, what does it matter, no one will see me in this dark. Stepping out of the pink slip, I remembered how I used to vacuum in my underwear while Adam slept. I said, "This slip is from a special shop. There they sell only lingerie. My husband bought it for me, he picked it out for me." This was a lie, since I'd bought it myself at Val-U-Village, which was across from the motel. It cost one dollar.

As I stood there naked with nothing left, I looked toward the flickering lights of the desert city's limits. And I thought of the people who inhabited the place, in their kitchens and bathrooms and garages and yards. I didn't know what they were trying to tell me with the lights that turned on and turned off. They made a pattern I could not yet discern. Why were so many people flickering lights for me to read? All I could tell was that the end was surely imminent. As I lowered my body to sit on the ground and receive it, all the trailers and houses went dim. Then the dimmed lights became stars, and those dull amber stars rose to the sky and then fell. I crouched on the ground, trying to gather the stars, which glittered darkly like jewels, or like pennies. I held some in my hands and found my way through the night.

Back at the motel, on the narrow but clean cot, I lay down for my first good sleep since winter. I put the star pennies under my pillow for luck.

When I woke what I believe now to have been many days and nights later, I did not understand where my dress was, and why my cheek was pressed into what seemed to be gravel. The manager stood above me, lifted my cageling arms into one of his grey-black t-shirts with an eagle on the back. He gave me some leather pants to wear. The pants were so heavy on my legs that I understood how we are all animals.

20

I let myself be sheparded into the motel office, where I took the phone and called Adam. When I heard Adam's voice rise toward me, I wavered and almost fell down. The manager spoke into the phone for me then, eyeballing me kindly for the very last time.

In my room I changed into a new pink dress, which the manager bought me at Val-U-Village. It had an elastic waist and sleeves like wings and it opened between my legs when I walked. I peered into the one-way mirror.

Back in the office I sat on the counter and slung my legs toward the manager, who stroked them. I turned myself toward the door. I fingered the money Adam had wired, and the dress, soft as light, and watched for the sunflower cab.

chapter four

Mrs Gold readied the outfit for wearing: a velvet dress, cotton tights and patent leather shoes as shiny as beetles. Ketzia gazed upon the preparations, which already found her in ruffled underpants. Downstairs on the kitchen counter sat a perfect birthday cake, marshmallow-frosted and topped with a single candle in the shape of a heart. "She hasn't stopped smiling since she was born," Mr Gold said to a figure in the hallway, invisible from the room, who cast a long female shadow over the changing table. "She smiles, but never talks." A woman's whisper: "Is there something wrong?"

As Mrs Gold wrestled a giggling Ketzia into the new rose-colored dress, Merry watched on, her mind on the presents downstairs at Ketzia's chair by the wooden kitchen table. She patted Ketzia's forehead with a heavy hand. "Little Ketzia," she said, putting her nose against Ketzia's own and pressing it down. "Little ugly baby," Merry said under her breath. Then, twisting thick braids onto her face like a mustache, she slipped out of the room. "Honey?" Mrs Gold called. But Mr Gold was gone from the scene. Ketzia stared at the ceiling, upon which shadows crossed.

Putting on a record of cartoon singing chip-munks, Mrs Gold spun Ketzia in circles. This was Ketzia's favorite game: when let go, she'd stagger toward the fancy wallpaper, recently installed by Mr Gold's confident hands. The paper featured ballerinas in pink gauze tutus that flared out from the wall—a brand new textile fashion. Looking closely, one could detect strands of gold and sil-ver woven into the paper which made it sparkle in light.

Ketzia, aware of the special fabric of her rosy dress and especially excited, spun toward the danc-ers, brushing against the wall again and again sent careening by her mother. She fingered the pink tutus, touched them with awe and with fear, as she touched everything, and as she would later a thin sliver of cake, the only one salvaged from the garbage pail's bottom where Merry's jealous toss-ing had put the confection.

Ketzia touched the girls on the wall without making a sound. "Good Ketzia," Mrs Gold said, watching with a distracted frown. "Good little one-year-old monkey." She took hold of Ketzia's arm and spun her again, spun her around pretty hard.

chapter five

A Riddling Tale

For a short but rather confusing time when I was younger, my sisters and I turned into flowers. We were left to grow in a window box all day, and only my sister was allowed inside at night. She had strong leaves and many blooms, like us all then, but hers were stronger, and more many. My mother kept her by the bedside to sleep, and returned her to our box for day.

One morning, as my older sister fixed the crystals for my mother's coffee before going back to the box, she said "If you come pick me this morning, and let me inside for the day, I'll never leave home for some man."

And so later my mother went to the window box and pulled her from the roots. After that, my sister wasn't a portulaca.

Here is a riddle for you. How did my mother know which one was my older sister, if we were three identical ground roses among the wandering jew? That riddle is easy to answer. My older sister had been indoors all night and had no dew upon her. She stood out in matte-red dullness.

An other riddle is harder to answer. My older sister married just one year later, leaving me and my little sister with my mother and her moods. Why?

chapter six

Hester helped the two girls swaddle into red snowsuits with hoods. Outside, they scraped ice into big plastic bowls. Ketzia held a spoon to her tongue where the metal stuck dryly. The snow was white, not grey yet from traffic. It was still coming down. When Ketzia looked up through street lights, the flakes looked like ashes glowing.

Back in the kitchen they slathered maple syrup onto the slush from a bottle the shape of a buxom woman. Fishing for maraschino cherries from a narrow jar, Merry exaggerated her mouth in a pucker. Hester—Mr Gold's favorite sitter from an agency downtown—cleared the plates with a laconic gaze. Ketzia noticed how Hester's long legs in lime cable-knit tights matched the lime of her cable-knit sweater. She watched as Hester crossed one thin leg over the other in a languorous motion, much like an octopus or bird. Under the heavy padded jacket and with a slight cold, Ketzia began to sweat.

"Stop that breathing noise," Merry admonished. "Stop that noise." Hester lit a cigarette and turned the pages of a fashion magazine. Ketzia padded out of the kitchen behind Merry, into the wood-paneled den.

There, sated with sugar, the girls watched television for hours, three entire programs: one about a little boy-like thing named "Harold"; one with the word "marble" in the title which had nothing to do with marbles, but rather with pen pals; and one that began with a group of furry, giant creatures in lavish colors hurtling down a slide, singing about "bananas." The unidentifiable animals caused Ketzia some concern, though the show was mostly pleasant, involving singing.

Later, Ketzia lay asleep on the dog's bed, her favorite spot, her sweaty hair matted in the snowsuit's fur cap. Merry slept on the couch in cotton underpants, cool as a cucumber in a garden.

Eventually, Mr Gold returned home from the hospital (where all the while their youngest sister had been pushing fitfully out, eleven strapping pounds of her, from between Mrs Gold's slender, pretty legs) and gave Hester a ride. The girls slept in the back of the car to their hushed tones and to Mr Gold's eight-track player, some song about a raccoon and a bible. It clicked heavily between sides.

chapter seven

Clever Ketzia

My husband was a boy I'd known since grammar school. Adam Brown was the smartest boy in my whole class. His family was special, too. In the summers Adam and Mr Brown rented out rowboats on a stream, like in a children's song. The Browns would not rent them on a day of bad weather or to boys who were not gentle. It's dangerous to put people near water unless they understand water. Adam knows this.

When we were five and six, Adam and I used to play chess on the landing of the staircase up to the third floor of his house. Or rather, Adam would play chess. He basically played both sides, telling me where to move all the pieces. This was difficult for me to do correctly so it was good I didn't have to make up the movements also. Adam's twin sister, Abby, would stand in a doorway and watch. This is the only time I ever saw her, really. After she whispered in his ear, he would say something like, "Put the knight two steps forward and three to the left," and I'd pick up the king or a pawn. "No, Ketzia." He was always patient. "No."

In junior high Adam got drunk with his best friend, Ivan. They drove a car across a lawn, chasing me and a friend. My friend was pretty and had been in a perfume commercial. We had tennis rackets in our hands and I threw mine over my shoulder as I ran. I remember very well the sensation of the racket leaving the palm of my hand. This weight, flung over my head, my hand empty and in perfumed air.

Later, when we were older, we went to several dances at the high school.

At some point Adam got it in his head that I was the smartest girl in the class and that the smartest boy should of course marry the smartest girl. I tried to tell him no—not that I wouldn't marry him but that I wasn't smart. This is something I know, I told him, you must believe me. But he would not. He insisted on continuing to date.

He brought me over to his parents' house for dinner one night after the movies, the spring of his college graduation. As usual, Mr Brown asked me to go down to the basement to get another two bottles of wine. He knew how much I loved to look at those walls all lined with bottles and bottles and more bottles, reflecting the moonlight that came through casement windows.

I went down to the cellar and felt along the wall for a string which when pulled clicked on an electric blue bulb. Mrs Brown hated the blue light. Mr Brown, whose wine cellar it was, said the blue made the cellar more exotic. I didn't like to touch the wall, which was always slightly damp. My hand clanked against something and the thing fell to the ground. I had passed the wine and hit a shelf full of trophies at the edge of the staircase, near its end. I looked closely at these huge brass things and saw they were all Adam's. Best of this, best of that, rookie of the year, player of the month, Short-stop Show Boy one of them said, I swear it said Show Boy. The trophy wasn't in the shape of a boy at all but that of a baseball glove.

I didn't understand how I had missed the trophies before. I hadn't even known they existed. This proved to me again how stupid I was.

"Stupid Ketzia, stupid girl," I said to myself. My mother used to tell me how smart I was, how pretty, how smart and pretty and pretty smart and pretty pretty. Just because, I suppose, no one liked me very much. And Adam's parents were worse. "O Ketzia, lucky Adam to have you. You'll make us proud proud proud."

I pulled down all the trophies. I didn't want anyone to have an accident like I almost had. One of those things could injure you. I laid them on the concrete floor and sat on the bottom step and wept. "Adam's so much better than I am," I thought. "If I had been more careless I might have hit myself on the head with one of his beautiful trophies and died. How can he think I am worthy of him? He'll never stay with me."

I'd always known my husband-to-be was of special talents but I hadn't known he was so talented that he had so many trophies he had to hide them in the basement. By the time I'd calmed down and thought "Adam is good, Ketzia is fine," I had forgotten what kind of red wine (and where on those rickety shelves it was) Mr Brown had asked me to get. I paced around furiously for several minutes when I heard Adam's voice at the top of the stairs.

"Clever Ketzia," he called down. This was a little joke we had. "Where O where can our wi-ine be?" He and his father loved their wine. "Wine and wine mix well," Mr Brown favored saying, "and never the two shall part." I cleared my throat and said in a low voice, "You'd better come help me Adam. I can't even remember the year. I mean vintage." So Adam came running down the stairs and what do you know, stupid Ketzia had left the trophies all in a row and he stumbled over them and broke an entire leg, I heard it sort of snap.

We got married that summer in a lovely ceremony in the backyard. A rabbi stood with us in a rowboat in the goldfish pond and the guests stood some distance away with great smiles on their faces. It was a sunny day for all.

Later, of course, Adam realized I was not so smart. "You are not the girl I thought I married," he said one day. "Yes," I agreed. "I am not myself."

And that was the end of that.

For a long time afterwards, I simply wandered. I went everywhere to see if I could find Ketzia again. *Jingle jangle jingle* went the bells in my head. I was so loud! I saw it on everyone's faces wherever I went, and I traveled far and wide. "Is Ketzia there? Is Ketzia there?" Never any reply. Sometimes I would laugh and laugh because I knew it was just that I am not so clever, after all.

"A Sunny Day for All"

chapter eight

L eaning back on her heels in the blue-tiled tub, Ketzia licked soap off her lip. She liked the sour taste, especially this bubble bath. It came in a pink plastic bottle with an image of a round face and nose. The girls had t-shirts with the thing on it that Mrs Gold had gotten with coupons, plus one dollar. They always wore them after two-girl baths.

In a rare and playful mood, Merry patted mounds of bubbles onto her chest, making a bosom, then helped Ketzia do the same. Merry was nicest to Ketzia in baths, especially with both of the parents there watching.

Mr Gold snapped photographs from outside the steamy room, as he did every Sunday. Ketzia eyed his reflection in the fogged-up mirror, an outline of a man. The girls stood for a moment and vamped for the camera, circles of bubbles on the bodies and piles on the heads as beehive wigs. They slithered their hands on each other's wet bodies.

As she knelt to rinse the girls with fresh water, Mrs Gold dropped a gold bar of soap. It slid out of the room and under Mr Gold's feet. Agile, he snapped a shot as he stumbled. Ketzia's favorite photo came out a monochromatic blur of blue walls, blue ceiling and blue towels, with a vague cloud of pale naked her in the center.

The girls stayed in the tub until their fingers pruned, the skin under delicate nails getting blue. In the end Merry's hair fanned like a mermaid's when she rinsed it—she always faced up, her eyes open and strange. Ketzia preferred to plunge hers in the water face down. By now the bath was lined with brown dirt.

Shivering as they stood waiting for towels, the girls heard the drain sucking water away and the camera, still faithfully snapping. The tiny square photos remain to this very day, framed in Mr Gold's office—a montage of nude girls on the wall.

chapter nine

You may think the life of a transcriptionist rather dull and small in this modern, visual time. But I find it leaves the mind free to roam hither and thither. Please, let me explain. After a string of troublingly 'social' office positions, I answered an ad for a typist for a group of private detectives. The ad described the opening in refreshingly simple terms: "Accurate, independent transcriptionist needed, good pay." They didn't want a 'self-starting people-person.' This wasn't a 'challenging job with lots of potential.' Fine with me. To be perfectly frank, my interest in office procedures has little to do with ambition.

This is why transcriptionist work at Triple D Co. has turned out to be perfect, with a perfect routine, perfect tone. The college-educated president founded the business after his wife left him for his father. The D's, he told me in my interview, stand for Depraved, Dishonest and Debauched, but my boss goes by Triple D because he always wanted to work in a factory. "'Triple D' has a factory feel," he acknowledged. When he told me about his factory-dream, I knew I had found a good home. Factories tend to be organized, and I like a routine.

I arrive at work every day with a steaming cup of coffee in a bright blue cardboard cup bought from the Greek deli downstairs. I sit at my station, adjust my headphones and boot up the system. Eventually, the investigators trickle into the cement-walled room. They drop their tapes onto my grey metal desk for transcription—usually uneventful narrations chronicling the non-goings-on of suspected adulterers, poor things, caught in entirely natural acts. Occasionally, an investigator will leave a handgun at my desk, then pick it up on his way out. I suspect that these handguns are not real. I assume the clients are.

Even after a couple of years I find the drone of the detectives' voices a comfort in my ears as I pedal away on the Dictaphone. When I hit a good rhythm I can type without stopping for very long periods, gazing out the grimy window until the city sun goes down. There is a maple tree in the alley and I mark the passing of time by its changing colors. The light falling down through its leaves makes me sigh.

When the day is done, I shut down the system and go home on the trolley. I listen to my radio headphones then, turned on to the public broadcasts of news, their soothing tones. This suffices to remind me of my investigating men.

chapter ten

Ketzia without Hands

I fell irreversibly in love with Adam when I was fourteen. That summer my parents sent me to live with an aunt in the city. I was being bad, they said. They said I was being a liar.

I had started to wear peacock-blue eye shadow and to fold my hair back with an iron, like wings. At drugstores I'd steal mascara. Instead of doing homework I would scribble nasty thoughts in a notebook, and leave it open for my mother to find. I shoved my grandfather's girlie magazines into my jeans, taking them home. I would act out the pictures under my bed, all alone. I'd often get found. And sometimes I would even skip my guitar lessons, going instead to a fried chicken place nearby. One greasy wing I would eat, and some water.

Unfortunately, on such a day my parents drove by the chicken place and saw me. I was standing outside in an alley, gnawing a bone, my guitar resting against a garbage can. They dragged me right home. "It's dangerous back there," my

41

mother said, panicked. "Ridiculous," muttered my father. But the very next week I skipped my guitar lessons again, and got caught by them another time. So my parents decided to give me to my richest aunt in a different town, for summer loan or longer.

The terms were clear. I was to work in the kitchen, mostly, which was not at all easy. Auntie Perfect, as we called her, had two sets of dishes in the house—one set for kosher and one set for not. Kosher was fancy and not kosher was pizza, cheeseburgers and stuff. Cleaning and arranging all the china took a great deal of time. Laundry took place in the kitchen as well, also an elaborate scheme. Every person in the house—my aunt and my cousins and uncle—had a certain color that was their own, like for underpants, socks, slacks and towels. But they were all various shades of grey that were difficult to distinguish.

Of course, I had other duties like mopping and scrubbing, polishing and mending. I had often thought that a very good fate for me would be as a scullery maid, so I settled in without complaining. In fact, I relished the labor. It provided disguise from a feeling of dread that had seemed to set in, as soon as I felt yearnings for Adam.

But the visit began badly, and never got less confusing. First, when I got to the city my aunt cut off all my hair without even asking. I had grown it my entire life, only trimming the ends off myself with nail scissors. It was brown just as it is now, but then it was very shiny and thick. My makeup was taken away as well.

My hair stuck out in all directions and my eyes looked small.

"If this child were *our* lady's child," Auntie Perfect said, "this child would still be a child." She stood me in the middle of the family room, naked with my shorn hair, and made dresses right onto my body in pale silk fabric. With a glinting needle, she never pricked me at all. The dresses, all pink, grazed my ankles and seemed to barely touch my skin—I floated inside them. The dresses she sewed had long sleeves that covered my hands. I had busy, nervous hands, and perhaps she meant to hide them. It was difficult to do my chores with my hands so concealed, but I adjusted as best I could. Soon, I left my body behind as if my eye shadow had been the glue that held me to the physical world.

There was the sensation all around me of judgment.

I found ways to escape, mainly into my head. Auntie Perfect's apartment was on the top floor of a skyscraper. Though I stayed indoors all the time, I gazed obsessively outside the windows, where there were many other buildings. On the rooftop of one were some dwarf maples and oaks. I memorized the arrangement of their branches with my brain.

I did manage to leave the apartment once to go to the post office and mail a letter to Adam. I snuck down a dumbwaiter, like I had read in some novel. In the letter I said, "Being apart has been difficult. I think I am in love with you and your black shiny hair. My soul is yours—though my body is gone and I cut all my hair." I thought when I got home I would set it to music.

I had no idea what I was saying at all.

Daily, after the housework was done, I just sat and stared at the roofs of the buildings, and at that slice of sky you could see between the buildings, and I imagined Adam flying through the night and entering one of the windows to take me away. He had shown me pictures of himself as a little boy in a superhero costume and this is how I imagined he would be dressed. Blue tights, blue shirt, red cape. A giant "A" embroidered on his clothes.

When I stood with my suitcase at the end of the summer, Auntie Perfect shook the letter I thought I had sent Adam right in my face. "This is the thanks I get?" she said, and stared at me. "Haven't you learned?"

"What?" I said. I didn't understand. "How did you get that letter?" I had dropped it in the mail, I was sure. I choked, realizing Adam hadn't received it. Still, I struggled in the silky dress to find my hands, so I could gesture 'innocence' and plead my case. But they were tangled in the fabric, gone. Then I heard Auntie say something about the children who would be given to me by God or not given me and then the train arrived. *Vas dos gut*, she said in Yiddish, and repeated it, *Vas dos gut*. She hugged me goodbye and ran her fingers through my hair, then trailed them far out through the air as though my hair were long again.

When I got home, Adam told my father that he was going to marry me someday and my father said "Fine." He used the word 'fine' to mean very good, I think. Finery. Fine, fancy, excellent. Or perhaps it was mere resignation. I started to wear lipstick again soon after, experimenting with silvery shades, metallic pewter.

Adam asked my father for my real hand in marriage many years later. My father said, "Why are you asking me? She's the one who has to answer." Still, I think this pleased him—I think we were all kind of hopeful for me.

chapter eleven

The Rosebud

There was once a poor woman who had two little girls. The youngest was sent to the forest every day to gather wood. Once when she had gone a long way before finding any, a beautiful little child appeared who helped her to pick up the wood and carried it home for her. Then in a twinkling he vanished. The little girl told her mother, but the mother wouldn't believe her. Then one day she brought home a rosebud and told her mother the beautiful child had given it to her and said he would come again when the rosebud opened. The mother put the rosebud in water. One morning the little girl didn't get up out of bed. The mother went in and found the child dead, but looking quite lovely. The rosebud had opened that same morning.

chapter twelve

Under the Christmas tree: a green plastic dish brimming with water, in which floated many pine needles. Ketzia trailed her finger in the water, lying on her stomach with her feet sticking out. The bottoms of her feet were white plastic soles attached to fuzzy magenta legs. It was Ketzia's favorite one-piece pajama; it zipped up the middle and had a hood. In the outfit Ketzia resembled a pitiful doll, but to her it was pleasure defined.

The demented family dog—for all intents and purposes Merry's dog, for Merry monopolized his affections quite fiercely—nosed under the tree beside Ketzia and stuck his face in the water to sneeze. She patted him tentatively. Ignoring her, he stuck his nose into the water again, and again sneezed, spraying water on Ketzia's face. Ketzia tilted her head away from the dog and looked up through the heavy branches, laden with ornaments that already had names, all characters from cartoons and books. They all had smiles and looked foolish. She looked at the lone glass angel that was nameless. It was sparkling and clear with no features. "That's mine," she said to the air.

Above her hung metallic balls, strands of tinsel, and a cardboard-framed photograph of herself last Christmas, nestled on the lap of a giant laughing Santa whom she remembered only vaguely, since the waiting in line to sit on his lap had been such a very long time, with too much talking around her, too many flashes of cameras and smiles. As it was obvious how little she'd enjoyed the adventure, Mrs Gold had taken Merry alone this year. They were at Shopper's Delight now, in matching red dresses, as Ketzia stood beneath the fir imagining a forest indoors, imagining the sky instead of a track-lit ceiling. Merry sat on Santa's lap that very moment, asking for a different sister.

"Hansel," Ketzia heard Mr Gold call into the forest where Hansel still had his face in the water and was snorting. "Come out of there, Ketzia," Mr Gold said, reaching under the lower branches and clipping a collar and leash on to Hansel. "Come for a walk with your dad." As Ketzia stumbled out from the tree some ornaments fell, but Mr Gold never noticed or minded such things. A Styrofoam star crunched under her slipper. Her father took another drink.

Dad led her outside in pajamas, despite the frigid air and wind. They walked down the block. "Hurry up," he commanded, giving Ketzia a start. As they watched Hansel weasel through the dirty snow, Ketzia felt a tiny scratch—deposited on her cheek from the needled tree—start to sting.

Ketzia was thin and getting cold, but remained silent by her father's side.

chapter thirteen

A word processor, strictly defined, is rarely required to think. Therefore, this might be considered a rotten profession for someone who when young was considered at least halfway intelligent. But I beg to differ. Despite my passive mind, via the machine I learn much about the ways of the world. In fact, I faithfully record many tales here at Triple D Co. that serve to wake up the soul.

For example, my men often are hired to spy on people whose injuries may not have crippled them so badly they cannot perform their 'jobs,' as they have reported to the agency that governs reimbursement for such conditions. Though garnering lost wages illegally from time to time, and therefore unsympathetic creatures to some, these suffering men, I believe, are deserving of tender feeling. Clearly, they are traumatized by the prospect of monotonous, non-physical employment. Sometimes the detectives fudge their reports, identifying with them. (For myself, I find it easier to record other people's thoughts than to initiate my own.)

The injured ones, dictations reveal, seem to remain at home, watching television much of the time, sinking deeper and deeper into insidious

depressions. When I figured out the difference between them and me—they only receive information while I am an information *processor*—I rec-
ognized the true dread of their existence.

Of course we also get our share, as you would
expect, of men and women suspecting their loved
ones of affairs. Usually, the suspicions pan out.
The logistics are far too complex to describe here,
involving often the most mind-bending systems
for sex. So, from the details I receive, I am able to
glean many sophisticated theories of war and desire. Because I have some experience with this
subject, it is very important that while typing up
these investigations I remain extremely detached,
no matter where my sympathy lies (though I must
admit, it lies everywhere). That is why I will not
go into great detail at present about my various
theories of lust. There is a lot I still have to read
on the subject, though I fear much is beyond my
ability.

Nevertheless, I am able to incorporate lots of
facts in my brain without even trying. In fact, my
keyboarding skills have improved so much that
now I can even read while transcribing from tape,
working two parts of my brain simultaneously (in-
putting and outputting). Of course, I feel somewhat guilty that I get paid to record these details
of suffering, which does nothing to help anyone.

On the other hand, I should confess this guilt
is tempered by a certain pride in my ability, which
is, you have to admit, of odd variety. And besides,
guilt is overrated, nearly as much as self esteem.

chapter fourteen

A Confused Ketzia Helps Grandmother

Once, when I was younger, I got home late from a guitar lesson and found my grandmother at the stove. "Grandmother," I said surprised. "Where's Mom?" "She had a temple meeting," my grandmother answered. "She's bringing home pizza for supper." My grandmother never came over without my grandfather, so I was confused. I was also lightheaded from my music lesson. I often got overanxious and held my breath during it.

I sat at the counter and cupped my chin in what I considered a girlish, contemplative pose. I decided not to mention Grandfather because I was glad for his absence, but unsure about why. Watching Grandmother open the oven, I caught a whiff of chicken. She was preparing for Rosh Hoshana. "O," I exclaimed. "Is there any crackling?" I loved crackling. Forget the diet. I ate a piece off a greasy paper napkin. "Mm," I said to ask for more.

"Ketzala," she admonished. "Leave some for your sisters! And the flavor may be delicious, but

53

you have to watch your figure. Otherwise, who else will?"

"I don't care," I said. "And Merry and Lucy don't know you're here." My siblings, who socialized a lot with the boys, were not home. I resumed the girlish pose and continued to watch Grandmother. A hush took over as she basted the chicken.

"What are you wearing to temple?" I asked, interrupting the stillness. "The same," Grandmother answered, meaning beige suit, long pearls. "You should wear that dress you wore to the anniversary." She was talking about a pink dress I had with pictures of mice all over it. The mice on the bottom edge of the skirt had real bows sewn onto their little mice heads, and when I wore it I wore a bow in my hair that matched.

"It's ugly, Grandmother." The outfit made me look so fat that if I even saw it hanging in my closet I cried.

I stretched out my hand, palm up, for more crackling. Every piece my grandmother gave me I popped in my mouth while still hot. I liked the electric feel it gave my tongue. There was so much that I had to stop after a while because of illness. My mother came home around ten and drank beer with a lemon. She and my grandmother leaned their heads together and talked. I heard my grandfather's name. Stern looks were exchanged, and stern voices, "...not allowed over," and such. I kept a tiny grin on my face in case they thought

I was listening, to prove that I wasn't. Then my sisters came home, aglow from their boys. I sat holding my stomach and watching.

My father didn't arrive until way after midnight. When he saw that the kitchen was full of people, fluorescence filling the hall, he got kind of mad. "Don't tire us out before the holidays," he admonished my mother. "The girls need their beauty sleep." He turned to me. "Don't eat so much, Ketzia." And to my grandmother, "Why are you fussing over chicken? What's the big deal?" He smelled of liquor, perfume. My mother looked grim and clenched her bottle of beer.

"Ach," Grandmother sighed, pouring some wine. "First you complain I never come over, then you get angry." "I'm not angry," said my father, taking a drink.

I just wanted everyone happy, in time for Rosh Hoshana. "It's a blessing!" I yelled, uncharacteristic for me. Everyone looked really startled. I rushed over to the stove and gestured toward the bird to explain. "Look, Dad, the beautiful bird! Giving us so much crackling!" I was bent over a little because I was so full. He stared at me like I was insane. "You love crackling, don't you?" I implored. My voice raised tentatively at the end of the sentence. "Go to bed, Merry—Hansel—I mean Ketzia," he answered.

"Doesn't he love crackling?" I pleaded, turning to my mother who shrugged, taking another beer from the fridge. This kind of thing seemed to happen often. That is, sometimes I forgot what was true, and what was just a feeling.

Witty and wise was Grandpa Sage,
He said, "I've reached a ripe old age,
But since I was a little shaver
I have been noted for my flavor."

chapter fifteen

Aside from the obvious ways I am suited to this employment—I type 120 words per minute, and, being extremely neutral of disposition, I am entirely trustworthy—I believe there are additional, more subtle compatibilities between me and the job. First, the atmosphere soothes me. I startle easily, and here, the phone seldom rings. Also, I have a subtle appreciation for the detectives' precision. They include addresses of every coffee or donut stop they make, amounts of change received at the tolls, and meticulous descriptions of every passerby who enters a scene. "Husband of client arrives at work, Building A. Wearing jeans, leather jacket, some kind of weirdo hat. Unshaven. Carrying a brown—no, black, yeah, brown—suitcase. Greets doorman. What a schmuck."

Perhaps I appreciate the minute details they relate because I myself keep a small diary of what I wear, what I eat, and what activities I have performed each day. When I get home after work (after stopping at the corner grocery store for a can of tuna fish or some sardines, or whatever I fancy eating that night), I sit on the back porch, which overlooks a rarely used playground. I believe it is rarely used because it belongs to an elderly home—a home my mother always referred to as "Death House" when we were young. As we passed by on our way to my grandparents', always an ambulance lurked nearby. These days, I sit and stare for a time at the metal and the barren trees. Usually I eat my supper right out of a tin, sitting there.

Then I go inside, put on a ratty t-shirt and jeans and read for a couple of hours in bed. Recently, I've been reading fairy tales. But before I go to sleep, before I forget to remember, I make a list of the day's events. It's quite full of details but I don't dwell on any emotion. I believe an individual ought to pay some, but not too much, attention to her life, and the surface of mine seems sufficient.

To make my list I drag a typewriter into the bed, although the machine is old and its oil sometimes stains the sheets. But I like the smell of typewriter ribbon—it reminds me of things, such as machines and men. The typewriter is of course a bit slower than the computer at work and loud, but the neighbors bear its shudders. I've explained to them how this is very good practice for word processing, my field. Working with a variety of equipment improves one's understanding of the variations among mechanisms—and organisms, I would hazard to say.

With electric you must pause more often, and wait for the return.

chapter sixteen

The Stubborn Ketzia

At times we were so very close. Once, Adam got his hair cut after having grown it past his shoulders. "Look how well I've shaved," he said. "I don't know how I did it!" "But you haven't *shaved*," I said. "You still have stubble from the weekend. You've only cut your hair." "Don't be disagreeable, Ketzia," Adam answered. "I shaved!" "No. It's simply a haircut." Adam touched my shoulder and leaned his forehead onto my own. "Shaving's hard," he said. "Say you like my haircut. Please?"

Later, Adam was in the shower and I was on the toilet. "Say it's shaved, or I'll drown you." "Do whatever you find necessary," I answered. "I still say it's a haircut." Adam's arm came from behind the shower curtain and dragged me under water. I had on all my clothes, though my underwear was around my ankles. He held me by the shoulders. "Say it's shaved!" I couldn't speak because of the water. Adam reached his arms across my chest. He tightened his hold. I struggled a moment and finally relaxed. Water streamed into my eyes and my mouth.

I stayed still a long time, in order to trick him. Then, I raised my hand toward his hair and made a clipping motion with my fingers, just like they were scissors.

chapter seventeen

That Saturday afternoon the family was gathered as usual at the grandparents' house. Old and tall and made of brick, it sat next door to the School for the Deaf, which was, much as you might expect, completely quiet. Through almost any window one could see students silently wander about the school's garden among roses and tulips, against an indoors-soundtrack of rushing faucets and voices.

In the kitchen, having a heated discussion as always, Mrs Gold and her mother did dishes. The water ran long and ran hard, covering their voices.

Mr Gold and Grandfather watched football in the den and looked at stereoscopes with their double frames. They chatted about money and women and sports, waiting for dinner. Soon, it would be laid out on the mahogany dining room table: hard-cooked eggs, dark rye bread, homemade borscht and tongue.

Ketzia and Merry crept upstairs to the attic, which was full of dirty pictures. Their grandfather had shown them his stash many times; often, when they visited him, he brought them there, but sometimes he was tied up with their father.

They each had their favorites. Merry, with her perfect curls and doll-like mouth, chose a collection of voluptuous bosoms—girls in satin pants and cowboy hats, girls on horses and motorbikes. Ketzia peered over her shoulder. "Get your breath off my body," Merry said. "What do you mean?" Ketzia asked. "I thought we were playing together." "Ketzia," Merry said sternly, "go away." Ketzia touched one of Merry's braids to try to appease her, but had her hand slapped off.

So, supplicating herself quite naturally, Ketzia crept over to the attic window smeared with dirt and grime. There, she pressed her face to the mottled window and watched the figures on the deaf school lawn, with their moving hands and motionless mouths. She mimicked them, pretending to sign through the pane: "Help Me!"

Lifting the top of the pink leather suitcase on which she'd been kneeling, she pulled out a pile of comics. "Want me to read to you, Merry?" she asked. Merry crossed her arms and narrowed her eyes. "Fine," she glared.

"Once upon a time there was a little girl whose parents died," the familiar story began. "She was sent to live with seven men. Her name was Fanny Annie." She turned the magazine toward Merry. There was a drawing of a girl in a red dress. She was roped to a tree. Two of the men held her legs in the air. Soon Ketzia and Merry heard footsteps on the attic stairs and hid the magazines fast.

"What are you doing up here," Mrs Gold said, flushing with anger. "I caught Ketzia looking at dirty photographs," Merry said. Merry ran to Mrs Gold and wrapped her arms around her mother's black cardigan sweater. "What are we going to do about her?" she whispered.

Leaning against the window and the silent boys and girls on the lawn, Ketzia willed herself mute. "I hate you," she signed to her mother and Merry, making no sound. She repeated the pantomime, feeling it louder inside. The words began in her head but traveled down, landing with a delicate spark in the pit of her stomach. Ketzia stopped listening to her mother and, pressing her lips to the window, she mouthed the same sentence against the pane. She felt cobwebs coat her tongue. Then, she swallowed hard, felt the sour taste in her throat and held it there a very long time, for what seemed like forever after, in fact.

chapter eighteen

Smart-Ass Lucy and Foolish Ketzia

My mother had three daughters and one was Meredith the Merry. Merry got married quite early. That left myself and Lucy. My mother liked Lucy the best. They were always at the mall finding smart outfits. Sometimes, I tried to help around the house. Ever since a child I liked to climb on the front of the vacuum.

My mother finally said I got in her hair one afternoon. She said "Leave me alone." This drove me away for the day.

Away means we lived in the suburbs and so I went to the city.

I rode the streetcar in and out of the city and in and out. Again I rode it in. The train stopped at the public gardens, I got off. At the wrought-iron entrance a magnolia-like tree carved in a pear shape greeted me.

"Come beneath my bower," the squat tree said. "Come cry in the dark of magnolia." The dark leaves shined.

"I annoyed my mother while she vacuumed," I cried. "You are not magnolia. Stop lying." Two dark shoes poked under. "Hello," a voice said. The tree shook and crab apples fell on me. "Hello down there," the voice said again. Lawyers walked through the park, theatre ushers and waiters. Hookers, students and winos. Salesmen and doctors. They all seemed kind. I wasn't afraid.

"Hello," I answered, unimaginative. The shoes didn't move, then went away. Biting one of the apples, I stood. The taste was bitter and dry. I took more apples into my pockets as a present for my mother. I resumed the walking.

At the edge of the park was an old bakery with a Hebrew sign in one window. Kosher, I think it said. "No-o," I answered the owner's first question. "No, unless cookies with my mother count, and boxes of cake." I was thinking of the brand with red and gold, their angel food. "Take some flour for your mother," the baker said. He handed me a brown paper bag. I didn't know if this was a joke or not.

"Ha, ha," I said, and took the sack.

When I came to rest later on a bench on a divided street, a lady asked why I was crying. "Because my mother likes my sister best, of course." Between the two sides of the street, small trees lined a sort of park. The park was a blackened statue and some lovely trash cans made of iron. A cold wind split the park. Evening. The lady shook her head and makeup moved sideways on her face. "Go home," she said. "Go home to your mother and don't contradict her."

"You remind me of my grandmother," I said. "But she never scolds me." "I can see why your mother likes your sister better," the lady said between crooked lips. "Is that any way to talk to an old *yenta?*" I felt ashamed. "No," I said. The woman walked off, carrying a bag from a bargain basement store. A pink feather boa trailed out on the ground. "I have that at home!" I called. I really did. Some change fell from her skirt or her hands, but she never turned back.

I thought about home. There, I had a diorama to build for science—it was to feature the progress of sunflower seeds from birth to harvest. Also, verbs waited to be declined: *je suis, tu es, il est, elle....* Prying up the old lady's pennies, I wandered west out of the city. The bells of the streetcar rang and I followed the sound, and followed the fast-moving traffic. The sun went down ahead, making lines of color across the sky, and I could feel the color upon my face like cosmetics.

I forgot all sense of purpose, fine.

When I finally got home, my sister and mother were unpacking groceries. I put the matzoh meal near some pink diet-soda cans. I dropped the pennies in the jar meant for change. My mother picked up the paper bag by one crumpled corner and threw it away.

"That's from that bakery," I said weakly. "From that nice man."

"Stop with the lying, Ketzia. Dirty, it is," my mother said. "Ahem," Lucy started, and left the room. "Sorry about before, I only wanted to help." I said, toying with my hands. "Hm? I can't hear you," my mother murmured, turning on faucets and clattering dishes into the sink.

In front of the television in the other room my sister meticulously painted her nails. I heard the noise and smelled the solution.

I crept outside. In the suburban quiet, our dog licked my calves as I sat on the front stoop. I held my math book open on my knees, something to do with division. With shut eyes, I could see the snakes and frogs and mice and cats crawling from every corner of the ceiling of every room of my mother's house, upstairs and down. But when I got inside, no trace of animals remained, except the sound of frogs and mice and snakes and cats in hiding.

We all got along better for the rest of the evening, but I didn't eat too much because my stomach hurt from crab apples. And I didn't do well on my math test the next day. I never have understood fractions.

chapter nineteen

K etzia crouched beneath the basement stairs. She adjusted her eyes to the dark. Before banishing her there, Merry had waved her hands before Ketzia's face. "I now render you blind, temporarily," Merry had said, adding that someone would be down shortly to mete out the pain. This is a game the girls often played, named simply The Punish. Punishments varied—getting bound to a chair and forced to witness the violent death of a doll; getting polio or requiring amputation, followed by 'rape' by a suitor; drinking ten glasses of water, and having a dictionary placed on the stomach, near where the bladder might lie. The game was played in the basement with its blood-red walls and brown shag rug, designed by Mr Gold for his darkroom.

Soon, Ketzia felt something creep up her leg. Maybe the punishment had started! She covered her face with her hands, almost too excited to look. Her blindness had worn off, so she kept her eyes screwed shut for a very long time before finally glancing down to see a sweet daddy-long-legs which had taken up residence just above her left kneecap. Amazingly, it sat on a small bruise Ketzia had suffered during yesterday's punishment game, which had involved a hammer and some complex insinuation that Ketzia was to be "locked inside

71

herself forever." The spider sat still on her spindly leg now, and Ketzia touched one of its own with affection—she identified with their little button heads, stringy limbs, pondering ways.

The basement door opened, throwing strong light down the stairs. "Where's my girl, my wench, my love?" Merry's voice boomed. Ketzia spoke. "Here I am, sir." Down the stairs Merry came slowly. "Where's my wench?" she boomed again. "Here I am, sir," Ketzia repeated, catching on. "Where's...my...girl?" And Ketzia, this time in a whisper, "Here I am, sir, here I am, here."

Merry bore down upon her. "What's this I see?" she said, pointing to the spider, which had not moved. Ketzia remained silent, unsure of the script. "Hm," Merry said. "How best to punish you properly with a spider in the way, on yesterday's delicious bruise, which today I was going to take the delightful opportunity to refresh?" Merry grabbed at the thing and shoved it in Ketzia's mouth before Ketzia could protest. "Chew, my pretty," Merry said. "Yes, sir," Ketzia said, muffled, feeling the tiny legs break in her mouth. Merry then ran up the stairs and slammed the door.

When perhaps hours had passed and Ketzia could hear Mrs Gold fixing supper upstairs—with the telltale sound of an electric can-opener running its lean blade along metal—she crept quietly back into the house toward the smell of sizzling meat. Merry looked up from the table, where she sat with the others. "Dad," she said. "Ketzia was downstairs again."

"Ketzia," Mr Gold admonished without looking. "Stay out of the basement, I mean it." Merry recommenced a loud hand-clapping song with Lucy as Mr Gold looked on with interest. *"The spades go two lips together, tie them forever, bring back my love to me! What is the meaning* (clap clap) *of all these flowers* (clap clap)? *They tell the story* (clap clap), *the story of love, from you to me!"* Ketzia tried in vain to join in, but this happy game was complex, and meant for only two girls, really.

chapter twenty

Ketzia at the Top of the Flagpole

Once my mother had to do some marketing and my father had to go to the barber and they left me alone in the house. For some time I had not been alone in the house, so I remember this well.

Though it was still light outside, in my bedroom-bordered-by-trees I could sense the dark coming. My room loses light fast. The house is colonial, painted white with black shutters. It communicates day and night through the walls.

"Ketzia," said my mother at the door to my bedroom. "Dad and I have errands to do." I looked up from a trunk full of doll's clothes. I had been sorting through my keepsakes. Many shining plastic bags, brimming full of junk, lay discarded on the driveway. I was all alone in life again, no longer with my husband. Why should I keep a wax candle in the shape of an owl?

I passed off a smile. "Good," I thought. "Goodbye," I said. My mother and father set off for the town square, and left me for the evening.

I closed the small red trunk and snapped its lock into place. I ran a finger along some ancient dents in the metal. Inside the trunk were handmade outfits, none longer than my forearm. A white terry robe with a thin terry belt, a black nylon bathing suit with a daisied rubber cap, a tiny evening dress stitched from red sequins stolen from my older sister's Halloween costume the year she was a nightclub singer. I had taken every tenth sequin to hide the theft. Merry had carried a battery-operated microphone on a rope around her neck. She sang, "You don't bring me flowers anymore."

How I had labored over those garments. Painstakingly! Unwashed and old but clean they were, folded in tiny parcels. I couldn't bear the sight, so I wandered to the kitchen and swept the floor. All around me, green-papered walls heralded evening, which dropped down along the inside walls and behind the green oaks, outside.

After I swept the floor I opened a window to let in air. "Dance, dust motes!" I said. "Proof of my labor!" A tiny bird came flying through. Green and yellow and blue, a special bird, domestic. I expected she had escaped from the old five and dime and I was about to suggest I return her there, when "Come to the square" she seemed to sing. She hovered near my face. Through her wings I saw colors that blocked my sight, again yellow and blue and green of rare variety. Although her wings flapped rapidly, I was not afraid. Animals carrying messages are important to heed.

I got a silver bicycle from beneath the house and pedaled slowly into town. I could not move fast because the bicycle was full of rust. Dominated by it! I rang the old bell (mute). The bird flew past me and away.

I knew the way to town. "Creak, creak," went the pedals.

Soon, I saw my mother's station wagon, silver and boxy and full of leather, parked calmly in front of the market. I leaned the bicycle against a lamppost near the library. "Library" was spelled out in black letters above the red door of the building. Around me bustled autos, people and wagons from the market, baby carriages and dogs and people carrying plastic bags on hangers from the cleaners and, in their hands, pairs of shoes from the "Shoe Man." I tried to make sense of the vehicles coming and going and I tried to find my mother and father in this crowd of people— and, as I did so, my head strained to return to the pink-ballerina-papered room with its green shag rug (like a lawn!) I had left for the square.

All in a dream, I looked for a vantage point and my eyes came to rest on an obvious place, that little patch of grass in the very center of all the shops— across from the deli, the liquor store and bank, across from the cleaner, the florist and the place where they sell stamps. There, a whitewashed flagpole stood among dimity flowers and buttercup.

I walked in my cut-off shorts and camisole and felt the setting sun on my legs and arms.

Slowly, the delicate hairs on my arms stood in the evening chill. My eyelids became like butterfly wings with the day's last bright and flickering colors. I knelt to gather some flowers. In childhood we brushed our chins and noses with flowers to show if we liked butter or boys. And if we liked both, which then better? Whichever one tickled more.

I crushed the yellow petals in my shaking hands.

The top of the flagpole was easy to reach. All I had to do was pass one hand over the other and hug the wood with my thighs. Up there I straddled the hot metal eagle that graced the flagpole. His wings were closed and he was enormous, larger than I'd imagined from below. The eagle was contained within his closed wings, and as I clung on he began also to contain me. I felt then this was my truest feeling, a sense of belonging with birds.

"Ketzia!" I heard my father's voice. He had his hands on his hips. "Come down, Ketzia," he said. "Don't be ridiculous and do what I say." "O no," I answered. "You're not getting me down that way again."

My mother came into view and asked me to get down. "No," I sang. "The other girls are married, and I'm all alone again. You just don't understand." She looked mad or sad and shook her head.

Next, my loner brother tried. I was surprised to see him there. Sometimes I forgot I even had a brother, because he was never around. That day, he happened through the square. "Ketzia," he said. "Just come off the flagpole." I shook my head. "Why not?" he asked. I lowered my voice and said each word on the same low note: "You. Know. Why." We had a certain understanding, even though I barely knew him.

Nearby, my sisters had their arms wrapped around each other. "Ketzia isn't right in the head," I heard them say in unison, looking at my brother. "It happened while you've been gone." He shrugged, and though he looked sad he just drove off in a brand-new red car. My sisters laced their hands around the flagpole and tried to shake it. "That's not going to work," I said flatly. They both walked away.

Night finally fell in a shiver. I lifted myself off the quiet eagle and slid down the flagpole. The square was empty and dark. I found my way home easily by listening for the crows. I imagined them in that midnight blue that matched their feather coats.

When I got home every door was locked. I knocked at the one we always used which was never locked, even when my mother and father traveled to the ocean or across the ocean. I heard my father behind the door. "Why should I let you in?" he said. "You wouldn't go down the pole when I asked you." He went back to bed.

Knocking louder, I heard my mother. "Why would I let you in, Ketzia, when you're such a pain?"

And then my brother. "Please let me in," I said. "O darling brother of mine." "Why?" my brother said. "You don't even know I exist." Yes I do, I thought, yet I did not speak again.

Finally, my sisters opened the door and, after lecturing me for a time about upsetting my parents and brother, we assembled some supper. We ate bread spread with butter and pastry stuffed with poppies. My sisters cried about how sad I seemed, and together we waited for broth to steam. The tenderness was surprising. In the broth were *knedls*, which my grandmother had taught us to pour in a bowl with no ladle. The number of *knedls* you got equaled the number of men you would marry, if you ate them. (I think it was a ruse to keep us all thin.)

By the time they were ready we didn't care to eat, being far too weary. We just went to bed with a peck on each cheek. I did have a taste of the soup, beforehand—so my lips were quite warm on their skin.

chapter twenty-one

The Star Talers

There was once a little girl whose father and mother had died and she was so poor she had no room to live in or bed to sleep in, and in the end there was nothing she could call her own but the clothes she had on and a piece of bread that some kind soul had given her. But she was a good, pious child, and when all the world forsook her, she put her trust in God and went out into the fields. There she met a poor man who said: "O, give me something to eat. I'm so hungry." She handed him her whole piece of bread, saying: "The Lord bless it to your use," and went on. Then came a child who moaned and said: "My head is so cold. Give me something to cover it with." She took her bonnet off and gave it to the child. When she had gone a little way, another child came along who had no bodice and was cold, so she gave it hers. Farther on, another child asked for a blouse, and she gave that away too. At last she came to a forest. It was dark by then and when still another child came and asked for a shift, the kind-hearted girl thought: "It's dark night. No one will see me. I can give my shift away." She took it off and gave it away, and as she stood there with nothing whatever left, stars began to fall from the sky, and they were shiny talers. Though she had given her shift away, she had a new one on, and it was made of the finest linen. She gathered the talers in it and was rich for the rest of her life.

chapter twenty-two

Husband and Wife

One night during our first year together Adam came home very late, and went right to bed. This wasn't unusual. "Don't ask me where I've been," he said. "Don't tell me what to do."

"Okay," I answered. "Likewise." I climbed out of bed, where I'd been already for hours in wait, and got dressed up. I left the darkened house and went to the local bar to ask about my husband. Entering from the rear, I edged past the pinball machine and down the narrow room. "Was my husband here?" I asked the bartender as I sat down.

"He was."

"That jerk," I said. I didn't really mind. "How much did he drink?" "Two longnecks," the old bartender answered. "Well," I said, and made a victory sign. "Give me two, and a shot of jack." I drank slowly, watching the clock. At last call I got another round.

When I got back into bed, Adam put his face close to mine. "Hello, drunkard," he said. "Want to see my underwear?" I asked. It matched my skirt. I pulled it off and flung it across the room before falling fast asleep.

"I'm a little drunkard," I forever after said, when I was cheerful and it was night, which was occasionally true.

chapter twenty-three

People don't believe me when I say that I prefer transcribing conversations to participating in them, but I do. In transcribing, unlike in conversing, it is possible to be one hundred percent accurate.

Perhaps it is the perfection of transcription I admire beyond the imprecision of talking, where I find too much potential confusion. Even if in perfect agreement with the one with whom one is speaking, often this is not understood. Alternately, if I type without error what a detective records, he can be sure I comprehend what he said—and not only comprehend it, but repeat it exactly. I believe many people (though not myself) crave to receive this kind of tender return.

I simply happen to have acquired the skill of communicating with my hands that which I hear. Others might too if only they would acknowledge how little need exists for the voice, or at least less than is commonly known. And this is also not widely known, but there are few things more erotic than typing. The feel of the keys on the hands, the task finished with a flourish of saving. The silence save light clicking, depending on the instrument used.

Besides, if I said out loud what I really wanted to say, I believe I would often make the sounds of a young chimp or a bird instead of a human. And who would hire me then? Surely it is best to murmur "Yes, sir," and resume my pleasant typing.

chapter twenty-four

Armless Abbelina

A dam's family was extremely sedated, which provided a good contrast to me. Mrs Brown was one of the most beautiful women— and so refined, with her black hair pulled back smooth and sleek. Mr Brown had a wit that could charm you to tears. Mr and Mrs Brown died very young, when Adam and I were still married. Mr Brown died of heart disease and Mrs Brown a mere two weeks later in an accident involving a row-boat, in their very own rose-filled backyard.

Soon after they died Adam asked Abby, his twin sister, to come live with us. She had lived at home with their parents until then. Adam said he could not bear the thought of Abby alone in the world. He thought the three of us would get along, that we were all alike and different in a way that would be pleasant. He thought it would be an unusual and creative arrangement.

And why should I disagree? Abby was as quiet as me. An artist, she spent all her time painting. Though I didn't understand her paintings I did find them lovely and disturbing to regard—full of all kinds of plants and animals you can't quite recognize that might be flowers or people, or just shapes from your dreams or nightmares. I said we should set a studio up in the shed in the yard. I even bought a portable heater for her.

Instead, Adam got Abby a job at the mall where he worked as well, saying she would be happier there near him, not painting in a shed all day. "She needs to get outside her head because it becomes very intense inside there," he said. Then he added, "Not like you, you know what I mean." "But I use my head," I said, confused. "I mean, shouldn't I be in the world more?" Adam seemed not to hear me.

So, right away I busied myself, tidying up the spare room to get ready for her. I dragged the space heater in from the shed. I hung bamboo shades on the windows. I even got her a glow-in-the-dark clock complete with a "snooze" option, and a paper Chinese lantern.

At the beginning things felt a bit forlorn. The first day Abby was with us Adam stood at the doorway ready for work, and kissed each of us on the forehead. "Goodbye for a while," he said to me. To Abby he said, "Take care of yourself, baby." I found this a bit strange, but siblings often have great bonds between them, especially brothers and sisters. I would have with mine, if he had stayed around, I think.

Later the same day Abby began work at the pastry counter in the mall. She called mid-morning to tell me she had been assigned cupcakes. "I mixed weird colors," she said. "I hope I don't get fired." But she needn't have worried—she called later to say her boss had given her a raise because they'd sold so many, not just a few more cupcakes than usual, but hundreds. People liked the moss-colored cakes, the lichen and the mustard, and her weird little images. "I don't know why I want it so badly," one suited man had said, pointing to an outlandish chartreuse and alarming canary. "But I do."

I called Adam at his department store to tell him. "Abby's special," he said. "She can't do anything the way you're supposed to. You'd better not call me at work again, though. It's hard to take a break. Christmas season, you know." Adam provided pleasant background music for shoppers on the piano, and his bosses liked it to be constant.

I climbed back in bed with a terrible headache. When it didn't go away, I thought I might be hungry and went to the kitchen. The cupboards were bare—it seemed all we had was a cheap muffin mix that came in a box. There was no milk, even, so I made the mix with water instead. It never congealed in the oven. I spooned hot batter into my mouth, but it was pretty bad and I couldn't swallow. As I gazed in the toilet, spitting it out, I decided to clean. First I scrubbed the bathroom with brushes, disinfectants and talcs.

Next, I went to the dining area, a particularly dirty room. The dust was so bad you felt it when you breathed. Pollen-heavy weeds grew up right through the floors, from outdoors. I looked around.

89

As a wedding gift Mr and Mrs Brown had given us some wooden chairs with hand-stenciled floral designs, made over a hundred years ago by some distant cousin of theirs. "Jewish furniture-makers are so uncommon," Mrs Brown had said. "Especially in Massachusetts," I'd murmured politely in response. The chairs were lovely, indeed, but covered with a filmy surface now.

I walked around the table and pushed each rickety chair in exactly six inches from the table. I slathered lemon-scented furniture polish from a can onto the seat of each chair and wiped it with a cloth. I ran my finger against the faded pink and yellow paintings of tulips that decorated them all, making sure I got all the polish off. While admiring my handiwork, I noticed that the spindliest of the chairs was askew, and as I nudged the chair in line with the others, I guess I unintentionally kicked the chair so hard it broke into pieces.

I sat at the polished table and watched the sun—a burning white globe—as it set through the curtains. I sat there a very long time.

When Abby came home with a box of cookies sprinkled with jimmies and saw the chair piled into a corner, she sat down across from me with a sigh. She pushed the cookies in my direction. I took an oblong one and scraped the sprinkles onto the table where they made a bright constellation. We stared solemnly at the broken chair and breathed in the smell of sugar and lemon polish. "That chair was really old," Abby said. "Was," I said, "and fragile." We shrugged.

When Adam and I were in bed that night he said, "What did you do to that chair?" "How do you know it was me?" I answered. He turned toward the wall. "Why are you mad?" I said to his back.

The next day, when Adam left for work, again he kissed the top of my forehead. "Goodbye, wife," he said with a smile. I slouched my shoulders casually. "Do you have any dry cleaning?" I asked, looking nonchalantly at the driveway where sparrows were gathered. Then Adam grasped Abby's arm tightly, and I watched their wide almond eyes meet. My eyes are a vague shade of grey—greenish-blue only when I'm crying or depending on what I'm wearing—and close-set.

They set off for work together in the chilly air. I watched their backs recede. Abby had on the uniform the pastry shop required, a short white dress that ended barely past her underpants. The bright white hemline drew attention to her legs, so lean and long in jet-black tights. She also wore a little cap. When Abby and Adam were out of sight, I stepped into Abby's dirty uniform from the day before and pinned the hem to make my legs look longer. Putting on black thigh-highs with a seam, I set out to clean Adam's studio.

Immediately, I noticed things were slightly rearranged. A tiny iron horse he usually kept on the top of his desk was hidden in a drawer. The old horse had been in the Brown family for generations, part of a miniature circus that had all but disappeared. Once, Adam had told me, there had been an entire carousel, even a little iron lion on the back of which had perched a miniature carnival dancer, a brown-haired girl in an emerald dress. "She looked like you, I think," he'd said.

It is too bad but as I went to put it back in the drawer, the horse dropped onto the ground, and as I stepped to retrieve it, my heel crunched down. I tried to hammer it back into shape, but the thing was so small and the hammer so large and unwieldy, I only managed to mangle the poor horse beyond recognition. I placed the metal on a folded napkin on the polished wood table and sat in a stenciled chair. I stayed there until the sun went down between the branches of a dead maple outside. For a long time, we had meant to get the tree removed, but we felt sorry for it and hadn't. We weren't sure what they did with dead trees, but suspected it was nothing good. I changed out of Abby's uniform and put on a brown dress of my own.

When Abby got home from work, she had a box of *ruegelah*. "They're not as good as your grandmother's," she said. She peeled one open and showed me the filling. "Too much cinnamon," we agreed. We ate in silence for a moment. "Adam loved that pony," she said. "That was his favorite." "I thought he liked the lion with the girl, who disappeared," I said. "O no," Abby said. "That girl is mine. She even looks like me. She rode the pony, you know. We called her Abbelina. Actually, I have her here!"

"O," I said.

"Once, Adam made her dance so hard her arms fell off," Abby said. "Then she became Armless Abbelina." I pictured Abby with no arms. Even with no arms she had a hold on Adam. Inside my head, I said goodbye to myself in an emerald dress, seducing a horse or a lion.

When Adam got home Abby and I were both close to tears, thinking about the broken toy. "It doesn't matter," Adam said to Abby. "If the horse were real I'd just eat it!" They laughed. I didn't really get the humor. Then Adam glanced my way, went into his studio and closed the door. He hammered out dirges on an organ until dinner.

That night in bed I was worried again. I smoothed Adam's hair off his forehead. "Abby has the green-dressed girl. She says she's Armless Abbelina. But you had said it looked like me." Adam closed his eyes. "No," he said. "Not really."

On the third day we stood at the doorway again. "You're getting too thin," he said to me. He turned to Abby. "Why don't you bring home some of those cheese rolls today?" "Hey, I'll walk with you," said Abby, and I watched them leave together.

My body felt tired all of a sudden. Slowly, I walked to our bedroom and took down Adam's overnight bag from the closet. I laid the bag on the bed and unzipped it. Inside I found a magazine, dog-eared on a picture of a lovely half-dressed girl. With long, full hair, she was wearing a costume that was a lot like Abby's uniform, except

93

she had on a peculiar straw hat instead of Abby's paper cap. The girl was very pretty.

I arrived at my parents' house a scant ten hours later—they had just put in a high-speed train. Adam didn't argue when I explained on the phone. "You and Abby are more husband and wife than we are," I said. "When your eyes meet, I am nowhere in the room. Please believe me that though I am sorry for the loss of your parents, I am also happy for you." Adam asked to speak to my father. My mother tucked me into bed with a wary expression on her face.

No one knew that I was pregnant.

I had a very bad sleep that night on my old twin bed, which tipped west as it always had. How my shoulder ached in the morning! Soon, though, I found it easier and easier to rest precariously on that bed for entire days in a row.

Sometimes my mother would force me out of there. Then, I would sit grimly in the passenger seat of her convertible as she drove to get my father's dry cleaning. "How do they clean it *dry*," I asked each time. "Explain it to me again. Something to do with chemicals?" My mother just stared at the road and didn't answer. I would repeat the question. She just drove right along without speaking. My mother loved driving. Even though it was winter she always had the convertible top down, and kept the heat blasting. "Dry cleaning?" I knew I was annoying.

Of course, soon the baby left me too.

I wrote to Adam. "Your wife has given birth to a child. His arms were golden up to the elbows, his bones were studded with stars, there was a radiant moon on his forehead and another near his heart." I tore the letter into pieces. "Your wife," I wrote, "has given birth to a half dog and half bear that she conceived with beasts in the woods." I mailed it that evening.

The following weekend Adam showed up with roses. He said Abby had left him for the department store owner, then left him for the pastry counter manager. Then, she had left him for no one. He thought she'd gone overseas, taking along all her paintings. I agreed to come home. It seemed that he missed me. Upon Adam's suggestion, before leaving we scattered the flowers he'd brought onto the lawn, in memory of the baby that never had been.

"A Lovely Half-Dressed Girl"

chapter twenty-five

Ketzia stood in the middle of the vast, wind-swept sandbar, eating a sandwich and staring toward the dunes where Mr and Mrs Gold sat in matching aquamarine chairs. Their skin shone with cocoa butter in the sun glare—it practically glittered as the Golds waved her way. Their hands were brown on the backs and pale on the palms from reading. "I'm a midget floating, I'm a midget!" Merry yelled at the sky as she bobbed in the water with her legs tucked in, a trick Mrs Gold had taught them. "Look at me," Merry yelled again and again. Mr and Mrs Gold had stopped waving and were reading their books with conviction.

They made a pretty picture, indeed, in their matching bathing suits patterned with American flags. They had on black sunglasses and cowboy hats. The girls' towels were nearby, weighed down with stones. Ketzia's had a chimpanzee photograph appliquéd on— the somewhat dim-looking chimp was eating a banana and scratching his head. Merry's said "Hey Big Daddy!" and featured a motorcycle and peace sign. The towels were set down on concrete near a ruined playground full of broken glass. The Golds always snuck onto the beach of the deserted mansion near the hotel. It was a dramatic location.

The motel where the Golds stayed had no beach, just a pool, which often had pee. They'd return there in evening and swim until chilled to the bone.

Sometimes Mrs Gold took them at night to peer in the windows of the mansion, and described dances that had taken place there, and courtships. A famous poet had worked at the mansion when she was a teen, and later—after an unrelated series of events—she had killed herself. Mrs Gold told this story with a distracted tone, gesturing, sometimes, toward the rusting swing set, which didn't figure in the tale. Then she would do an abstract ballet on the concrete to represent 'courtship' and 'suicide.'

Now, Ketzia squatted in the sand and dangled a piece of bologna in the warm, shallow water. She licked it for salt, and dangled it and licked it again. Her bathing suit was a two-piece concoction with a thick strip of clear plastic connecting top and bottom—an odd, recent fashion. The top and bottom were made of pink terry cloth and were soaked to the skin. The plastic over the stomach heated up in the sun and trapped water there. It was strange, like an aquarium of skin. Ketzia stuck the bologna on the plastic and wiggled a bit, and it stayed.

She ran laughing to Merry in the water, flew onto her back and said "I'm a midget floating with bologna!" Merry paddled away. "You're weird," she said, and ran to shore. Ketzia squinted out to the horizon, distractedly nibbling the edge of the meat, proud of her ability to float and nibble simultaneously. She hadn't heard.

chapter twenty-six

The Synagogue

I always loved the clang of the streetcar and often rode it just for fun. One time I went from my parent's house to the synagogue at a streetcar stop in the next town. At the four corners of the intersection were the synagogue, a diner with blue-checked tablecloths, a Persian Rug Store and Chinese Buffet. I climbed off the trolley, walked cautiously over the tracks and headed toward the temple steps.

Inside it was empty, being a weekday. I was alone in the sanctuary, so sang.

> *O holy temple,*
> *Please get me a man.*
> *One who will have me,*
> *One with long hair.*
> *If I can't have him here*
> *I'll jump off a weir.*
> *O holy thee.*

I noticed a rabbi standing behind the giant ark the whole time I sang. He didn't step out until I was done. He spoke somewhat sternly when I finished my song.

"That's no way to get a man," he said. He had piercing blue eyes, like a cliché. He stood against the ark which, quite contemporary, had red and orange and pink abstract stained glass Hebrew letters upon it. The ark glittered inside with silver and scrolls. It was lit from all sides with large candles. The rabbi's eyes glittered too.

I became somewhat self conscious. I wore denim slacks and a hand-me-down blazer that used to be my brother's. Its sleeves were too short and it had leather elbows. I tightened it around my waist and clung with my hands to my sides. Why is it always so freezing in temples? "Why?" I asked out loud, about not getting a man.

"Look at your hair," he said. "Not even blonde but bright yellow. This isn't the place to look for a man, my dear child." My hair did have at the time a marigold look, unflattering to the complexion. I'd gotten the color from a store. It brought out the greenish tone to my skin, so my head was like a bright, silly flower on top of the stem that was my neck.

The rabbi was handsome, just my luck. Another man to see me as wrong. The boys at school thought I was a loon, or so I assumed. Recently, a boy had groped me in the cafeteria line and said "Goldy, you have a tight ass." I hadn't any response at the time, and fled the scene. Now, I stared the rabbi down.

Despite being handsome, he wore a pointy-collared ribbed sweater and wide-legged jeans. Aha, I thought, my way in. Even though I was insecure, I knew I was pretty. "Ibbity-bibbity nerdy turd man. *Please* do your job and tell me I'm fine." I put my hands on my hips and angled them toward him. I was becoming light-headed, something that happened when I misbehaved. The rabbi answered "You won't find that here, my dear. I'm afraid you won't find that here." He cast a kind glance at my forehead.

"You mean because it's a temple of God? Not a temple of love? Or because I'm a blonde? I'm not really a blonde!" I leaned my head forward and showed the roots. "I'm a brunette. I'm just this dumb girl. I'm not even Jewish." This last was a lie, despite my mother's Christmas trees. I went on and on without breathing. Then I finally started to cry.

The nerdy-turd rabbi tried calming me down. My outburst had done its work so he could do his own. First, he sat me beside him in a tiny office with many books. He gave me milky tea. He was fatherly, sort of, and told me a story about some woman who was a queen and how "she, who required nothing, had in that very way obtained favour in the sight of all of them that looked upon her." Later, she had fasted for many days to save others.

I puzzled over the details while I pulled blonde strands of hair over my eyes. I tried to judge how long it would take until the blonde disappeared. The rabbi and I discussed appropriate methods for obtaining a spouse, positing the primary goal not as acquisition but self-love. "I'm just not right in the head," I said. He seemed to agree. I told him I was scared all the time and didn't know why. He said he was willing to talk with my parents, but, of course, I declined.

On the streetcar home I vowed to fast, and thought about how the afternoon had been moving. I thought maybe I was getting close to something important. But I felt as alone in the end as I had in the beginning. Still, for quite some time I'd take the streetcar back by the temple and think about that man, the letters imposing behind him.

It was a phase, I suppose.

Some months later my blonde was gone. Back to the brown! And like a bulb I went underground again, thinking vaguely of fear and of men.

chapter twenty-seven

This job keeps me rather serene, a state that I currently relish. The workload, never too much for just one word processor, offers me the luxury of keeping the tapes on a natural speed. Transcriptionists don't always have that option. In other positions, where one must answer multiple phone lines, fax and scan—all kinds of contemporary tasks—it is often required to turn up the speed dial. Then the dictator's voice sounds like a squeaky cartoon with a frightening tone. In jobs like that my fingers would shake.

I like strict transcription because it is steady. The flow of words to my brain remains in control.

There are very few drawbacks to plain old transcription, in fact. Stiffness in the fingers in rainy seasons, for example, and aches from repetitive motion. Also, some days my private investigators sit in a back room lighting cigarettes and drinking. I enjoy the smoke and liquor-scent, but their voices interrupt me some. I like nothing worse than overhearing too many voices at once. It is similar to seeing yourself in the mirror alongside a friend. I have met others who find this disturbing.

It might look as though I am a recluse, but this isn't the case at all. In fact, I used to live with someone, and I liked him very much. But I was sensitive to so much proximity, I think. I believe many people suffer from this condition but will not admit it.

To modulate the predicament, which can arise despite this most impersonal and pleasing job situation, I tend to keep my headphones on even in the absence of work. The detectives often invite me to join them, but I gesture toward the ears and computer. I play some kind of sound—I quite like blank electric static—and prop up a book I've been reading. Transcribing its pages, I practice my fingering. This brings on the sensation of calm.

chapter twenty-eight

Monkey Dance

Though at first in our marriage I was terribly shy—practically frozen inside my body—eventually I learned to dance like a monkey, to dance like I was on a table but a monkey, not a girl. Adam liked it. He was always encouraging me to be more wild, being a bit wild himself. But in the beginning I was too timid.

When I first moved in I made cautious housekeeping changes—tidying pillows, dusting the sills, scraping old mold. Yet soon I became a lot bolder. I had always felt the imperative of beauty, but didn't have the guts to apply it. Slowly, I began to transform the house cheaply, within our budget. A beautiful home will reflect our beautiful souls, I told Adam.

I had few ideas of my own, though his neighbors had unusual taste which I borrowed—ceramic reindeer, plastic bunnies, windmill daisies. I bought silk sunflowers and covered the ceilings of closets. I peeled up rugs and painted the floors green—shades of pistachio, olive and bottle. In my own hair I had streaks of green, subtle but there in the brown, one of my few unusual features. Adam got green-sick so I left his study brown, much like the plains where we lived. I stapled tumbleweeds onto his wall.

None of this was artful, I fear. But our house *was* crowded with nature, inside and out. I'd shoved seeds in the ground and they soon would sprout, and I'd buried bulbs that were sleeping. I worked in a new kind of frenzy, weeding and planting. I was the same old Ketzia, awkward and shy, but my limbs felt gangly and excitable digging in dirt.

One day, making small holes in the soil for pink plastic flamingos with borders of moss, I discovered a cigar box full of jewelry. A dancing monkey graced the top on peeling paper, and the inside smelled of patchouli. I felt my stomach drop with intuition. "Whose are these," I said, holding up feather earrings. "And these," holding up three silver rings. "I wasn't hiding it from you," Adam said when he got home. "I just wanted it where we'd never touch it." He stroked my ears and put it back in the ground.

But that night, and for many to follow, I dreamed of poor monkey, buried and sad.

Eventually, some neighborhood boys came knocking. They needed money, they said, for baseball. That way, they wouldn't run the streets and fight. They wanted uniforms, appliqués, sneakers and bats. The boys were selling chocolates. I never could say no to boys. I said to follow me and I led them to the backyard, where flamingos surrounded sunflowers, all within spirals of moss. "There in the ground," I pointed. "Stuff you can pawn." I was tired of waking up crying. When they found the tin, the boys ran with the jewelry and dropped all the candy. Furtively, I ate and ate, pacing among the flowers.

I had eaten twenty boxes of sweets when I began to feel very dizzy. In fact my head began to glow and pulse. I'd never eaten so much. Becoming afraid of what I heard in my head—words like *skatesoul parade* that didn't make sense—I crouched on the ground. But soon I had more energy than ever. I decided not to waste the candy foil, so I cut the shapes of flowers and triangles and circles and squares, diamonds and hearts and one tiny bear, and hung them around the fence of the house. When Adam returned, he saw what I had done. Sunset light shimmered through the holes and cast beautiful designs on our shabby house. "I bought them, sort of," I said.

Adam smiled. He knew it was garbage. "With what money?" he asked. I kicked my feet in the ground in a way that I thought might appear casual. "Just with the stuff you buried out back"—I thought if I said it that way—"I didn't touch it, though, just like you asked me." It was true I had pointed the tin out to the boys, not given it to them with my own hand. In the hard glow of our neighbor's flood light we stared at the decorated chain link fence in silence. We ate dinner without talking, too.

"Why did you think it was fine?" Adam asked around midnight, pouring more whiskey. "You only told me not to touch the stuff," I said. "You should have told me not to give it away." I tapped my foot impatiently. The sugar was taking its toll. Mixed with whiskey, it muddled my brain. I tried to make a jingle on the floor.

Forgive me, 'give me Adam Brown,
The tin's my sin but you're my frown.

"Look," I said. "I think we can get the box back, if it's that important to you. We'll find those boys. They live where that broken car lies in the yard."

Adam shrugged. "All right," he said. "It's not my choice for a Friday night. At least let's bring the whiskey." I got a flask from the pantry. Adam set out the door. I fell behind. We walked to the park where the boys often hung out with their skateboards. We passed the flask back and forth. Once at the empty park we decided to wait.

Tired of standing, I found a tree that was short and climbed up it. Hiking my dress around my waist, I knew Adam would get a glimpse of underpants. I kept a sly eye toward him. The sky was sort of violet-black, streaked with grey, and the grass extremely green. Adam followed me and together we sat in the tree. I had my mouth in a nervous grin. "Get off my face," I thought. "Get off my face." My smile was the sickest thing I'd ever seen.

After not very long, the boys showed up, the boys who'd asked for money so they would be in their homes at night. And there it was, pitch dark and the little good-for-nothings playing in the park. I had no patience for liars.

The boys stopped under our tree and made a tiny fire. I smelled hot dogs. I knew Adam would be angry they'd wasted his trinkets—or rather those of some girl—on cheap wieners. Peering down, I saw a boy with the meanest face. I grabbed Adam's elbow. I thought they might attack us with bats, but instead they all ran away. We jumped to the ground. We each ate a hot dog and then walked home.

"Jesus, Ketzia," Adam said at his house, dark circles under his eyes. "Please let me sleep. I have to go to *sleep*," he pleaded. We'd drunk a whole lot, it was true. He went to lie down.

I became sad. Going to the yard, I knelt on the grass. After the terrible fiasco with the patchouli tin, I resolved to make everything perfect. A song came into my weary head. "How perfect we will be when I'm through, how perfectly me and you. My monkey boy, my! you're a joy. I love you and you and you." But singing always made me depressed, and getting depressed always made me tired. I fell asleep on the lawn.

Waking later, I stared down at my half-naked body. "Is that really me?" I thought. I went to our door and stood knocking. When Adam answered it, I asked him if this was home. "What?" he said, confused and half-drunk. "Yeah, you're already here." I remember thinking well, if I was already there, who was the one standing outside? I got scared, and scratched my head and ran away. I wouldn't go back until I understood. It was near dawn by then.

Near the park I saw the boys from before, but they had become a thousand. In the ball field lights they rose from the ground on delinquent boy-toes and lifted into the sky. From above they looked me up and down, my lack of clothes, and smiled. Leading me to where acres of dandelions had grown, they spoke to me very sweetly. "Pull these up for us," a simple request. "Damn you," I said. "You know I will do what you say." I was a coward and couldn't defy them. I crouched on the ground for hours. I weeded over five hundred flowers, though it went against my nature to kill them. I got so much dirt in my fingernails that they started to bleed.

Finally Adam showed up to save me. "Sorry I was so hard on you," he said. "The boys made me do it," I sobbed. "No," I revised calmly. "I did it myself, because they're not real." Adam lay down. I heard him speak from the green. "Are you going to be real or not? I kind of need to know." After only a very short pause I, who have no sense of tone, decided to seduce my boy with beautiful song. At the time I was too afraid of being alone.

"I could be real, eerily real. I'll reel for you my Adam," I sort-of-sang in a gravelly drawl. Around the playing field I loped around, propelling myself forward with really loose limbs. It was a kind of monkey dance with gangly arms. "If you

114

were on a table we'd be richer than rich!" Adam exclaimed. "Only if the men were all monkeys!" I yelled. "Only if gorillas had wallets!"

After that evening I became somewhat more confident and strong. I got rid of the boys in my head and seemed to settled down. I kept our house tidy and didn't get too confused, so we were happy for a while, of course.

"You Know I Will Do as You Say"

chapter twenty-nine

The Fox and the Geese

Once the fox came to a meadow and saw a flock of fine fat geese. He laughed and said: "What luck to find you all together! I'll be able to eat you one by one without wasting time." The geese cackled in terror, wept and wailed and begged for their lives. But the fox was unmoved, and said: "There will be no mercy. You must die." Finally one of them summoned up the courage to speak. "If we poor geese must lose our innocent young lives," she said, "grant us but one kindness: give us time to say one last prayer lest we die in sin. Then we shall line up in a row so you can pick out the fattest every time." "Very well," said the fox, "that is a proper and pious wish. Go ahead and pray. I'll wait till you are finished." The first began a long-drawn-out prayer that went "Ga! ga! ga! ga!" over and over again. And since she went on and on, the second, instead of waiting her turn, started in with her "Ga! ga!" The third and fourth followed, and soon they were all cackling together. (Our story will resume when they have finished praying, but for the present they are still at it.)

chapter thirty

There are days, as one might expect, when I lose all passion for typing. My fingers simply go slack at the keys. They begin to feel paralyzed, as if they have no will to live. It is then that I listen to the drone of the men with the exact horror one experiences at the shock of sudden boredom with a lover. Their voices, which I generally receive with utter kindness, become complete irritants to my ear. Why so? It is difficult to say.

I cannot trace these unpleasant days to unpleasant evenings preceding; neither can I trace these days to pleasant evenings preceding which have rendered the day-to-day displeasing. My evenings, as I have indicated, are neither pleasant nor unpleasant regardless of content. After activities of a sexual nature I do feel a certain new sense of color, of sound, a feeling of having been chosen for something extraordinary in time. But really I can concoct this sensation out of even the most banal romantic exchanges with strangers.

That is to say, I fall in love quickly and unpleasantly, with a feeling not unlike that predicting a brief but passionate illness, such as the 24-hour-bug, and it usually lasts as long before I move on. It is all in the mind or the gin.

On the other hand, perhaps this 'desire' *is* connected to the days on which my transcription loses all nerve. Because if a long time passes and I don't have the illusion of love, I begin to miss sorely that strange, smug and often wholly impersonal satisfaction that comes from being wanted. It can render the rest of the world agreeably incomplete. In fact, I can type brilliantly for months after just one night of passion, feeling no loss of the rest.

But if a long time passes between such events, it is difficult not to slump at my desk when I slide a new cassette into place. As my foot clicks it on, there's no thrill from the words, only the sense of their bodiless sound. During those periods I have to rewind and rewind simply to hear the thing and get it correctly down through my hands. Yet, with some violence to myself—an internal slap on the cheek, 'Who do you think you are, little miss transcriptionist'—I get back into the swing of things, back into my job as a typist.

chapter thirty-one

Choosing a Bride

Adam always was nice to girls, including me. He sure knew how to play us; next to baseball and piano we were his greatest talent. Even when I was with him it was lovely, really. He had many charming tales of affection.

For example, he told me about how, when we were young, he didn't know which of the Gold girls he liked best. This is when he was only four or five. He was sort of a prodigy, in every way.

As the story goes, there were three of us—I was in the middle. We are all, I am told, as beautiful as the others, though we became beautiful at different times and in different manifestations, as is the way of girls. We were like one person but also unique. This is best exemplified in the style of our hair. Our heads are all the exact same shape and size, but one of us has loose amber curls that lift and fall in delicate waves, one a blonde headfull thick and straight, and I, fine brown strands that bend strangely this way and that.

When we were kids, we often played "The Giant Rings of China" on the driveway. This game was based upon a magic trick we had seen in an auditorium at my grandfather's temple. There, we were served carrots and olives and tuna and cake. After the trick the magician chose my older sister from everyone in the audience to give a caged rabbit, for her to keep forever. In the Giant Rings he did something involving fire. Then we walked down a long cobblestone hill to get home, along the trolley tracks from the city. I can't remember the rules of this game at all. It involved us jumping through hoops Adam held.

Our other game was called "Merlin's Floating Ball." Adam's job was to throw a clear inflatable ball at each of us and we would bat it back to him. We'd play it for hours. Adam also taught us to play "Occam's Razor" in which he spun us around and made us stagger. My brother acted out the part of 'razor,' standing stock still in the driveway, arms held straight by his sides. He was always so willing—o how I miss him.

Often, after we played my mother would invite us in for a snack. In the beginning this was thin-sliced orange cheese, individual slices in cellophane paper, set on a plate with franks from a jar. When we moved to a bigger house she served us something paler orange with red wax lining. The cheese came wrapped in string, like netting. Finally, when we were grown, she placed the cheese out on a blackboard tray and scribbled on Italian names.

Later, Adam always said the reason he chose me was how I ate that middle cheese. My older sister would eat everything, rind and all. My younger sister took some care to remove the wax but not enough care. She left pieces of cheese with red lining all over her plate. In preparing *my* snack, on the other hand, I always removed the wax neatly. I didn't take off too much and I didn't take off too little.

"And that's why I married you," Adam said when we were older. "Tell me again," I'd say.

All through our marriage, as something to do to feel useful and alive—as one feels feeding animals found in the wild—I made all of our meals. Adam especially liked lunches. For him I perfected grilled cheese. He didn't make much money at piano, so we never got fancy cheese. For fun instead I'd cut shapes out of the sandwiches to please him: symbols, tulips and hearts.

chapter thirty-two

Early on, when lonely, Ketzia developed the secretive habit of picking her nose behind the pages of books. An obsessive reader, Ketzia left few clean volumes both on the Gold shelves and on those of the local library, through which she methodically mined. Of course, when accused she'd deny it.

During one very bad year, full of various confusions, Ketzia bicycled there from school and hid from view whenever at all possible. The Golds would have preferred she spend the rest of the time as 'normal' children did, 'playing,' as it was called. And she was also supposed to practice guitar. "Why don't you call a friend?" Mrs Gold repetitively said when Ketzia would slink home, arms full of books, or "Don't you have music to practice?" "Okay, mommy," she'd say, and scurry upstairs to her room. Once there she would hide in the closet for hours with books, her heart beating fast, afraid Mrs Gold would come in. She kept the guitar in there with her, perching on top of it. Because it never got played, what would it matter?

Finally, after working her way meticulously but rapidly through the Children's Basement—from alphabet books to zoo animals—Ketzia was allowed upstairs where the adults sat, among medical encyclopedias with entries on "Reproduction of Mammals," dictionaries with words like "intercourse," and any number of Russian novels. Entrance to the adult room was very exciting because it was quiet and serious there. It had been too noisy downstairs with all the joyful boys and girls colorfully rendered on so many pages, shouting at her.

But really, reading anything at all provided Ketzia with a sort of thrill, much like the thrill she got imagining herself the recipient of some deadly bad news—her music teacher, for example, suffering a terrible fate, after which was discovered a filthy letter written to his young prodigy, who, after learning of his death became suddenly mute when questioned about the circumstances of his demise, to which she had been privy prior to the accident—and so on, and so on.

Little did Ketzia's parents know that, busy hands hidden inside a paperback novel, Ketzia was in fact in an adult sexual thrall that, later in her life, would attain its own epic proportions whenever she lay in bed beside a distant lover—the kind she gravitated toward. She had precise methods, in fact, with which to distract herself from their cold being.

Lying there, she'd remember the books, the nose-picking. Then, to distract herself from the oddness of that, she'd compose elaborate scenes in her head wherein she was informed publicly of the men's untimely deaths. Next, to hide her guilt, she would burrow into them hard—surely they deserved this last, final comfort before she would leave. But her intensity confused the men, of course, since often they had made her acquaintance only that day. With strange frequency and coincidence, many of them—previously unmoved—found themselves saying things about flowers or birds, and the passion not being returned.

Such the unfortunate trajectory Ketzia's nose-picking habit took from fifth grade through her marriage, though it was of her own design and rather to her liking.

chapter thirty-three

In the absence of emotional bonds, I have made a commitment to expanding my imagination. As part of this endeavor I offer myself visionary exercises; today, I considered the idea that it would be nice if we were born as flowers. At night I have been reading a touching book called *The Flower Children*. In it the author has written short poems about little flowers, who take on various personalities. For example:

> *Thirsty little Buttercup*
> *Caught the dew and drank it up,*
> *Said cool water was so good,*
> *She didn't seem to care for food.*

The book contains colorful renditions of flowers-as-children, with sweet faces and pastel clothing, save one ominous drawing of a lurid old man.

A guy bought it for me one day when we met by literally bumping into each other at a used book store. He was leafing through *The Flower Children* and dropped it when we crashed. I picked it up and he blushed, quickly saying he found it disturbing because the flowers—though children—had flirtatious glances. I told him that I found the book erotic, to put him at ease. After that I stayed at his place several times. He reminded me of my brother, I think. He was about twice my size, and very kind. He had a successful career as a gardener. Although I prefer to keep my life free of entanglements, finding them a distraction from my trade (to be an excellent typist, I must keep my mind completely clear), I was interested in him. He seemed completely sensual and complicated.

One night a couple of months after meeting, we drank a lot of gin at a bar. The detectives were going to a convention, where they would purchase all kinds of surveillance devices—phone taps, voice scramblers, cameras you could hide in your tie— so I had the next day off. After five or six gin and tonics, he told me a story about his life.

It turns out that his mother had been quite depressed and one night his father found her walking around the neighborhood naked. The father had a bad temper and tied her to the front stoop even though it was freezing outside. When my friend left the house for first grade the next morning, he had to walk by his naked mother, whose tears had frozen on her cheeks. And when he got home from school, his mother had disappeared for good. I cried pretty hard when he told me the story. It had been a long time since anyone had talked to me so personally.

From the bar we went back to his place and there I told him some things about myself too, about wandering around the desert and my visions. It was a good thing I had the next day off, because when I woke up I had a terrible hangover. After that night, though, he completely stopped returning my calls—but it's just as well. I am very busy with my work and with my self-improvements.

For example, in the lag-time this week I have been transcribing those poems and considering how lucky we are to live longer than flowers, even if not much happens to us.

chapter thirty-four

The Tiny Closet

For some time our marriage was uneventful, perhaps even easy. But on our first anniversary Adam gave me a huge string of keys. "These are the keys to all the rooms of my house," he said. "But do not open the tiny closet at the end of this hallway, okay?" This seemed odd because I thought I knew everything about Adam. We had lived together for over a year. I wasn't aware of any locked doors and besides, I would never have considered opening his things. Suddenly, though, I was overcome with a desire to see what lay inside that closet, wherever it was.

"Ketzia?" Adam said. "Okay?" He had a way of making commands into gentle questions. I said of course I wouldn't look—after all, I said, I did have secrets of my own. I put the string around my neck, and the bell-like sound it made reminded me of our private understanding.

Yet I began to sit at the end of the hall next to a tiny door I found there when Adam went to work, my hand on the key around my neck, fluttering it against my collarbone. My head would lurch with fear when I heard his car pull in the driveway and I'd run into another room and fling open a book, smile demurely as he entered, and feel stricken with guilt for something I hadn't even done.

Eventually Adam had to go on a short trip to inspect a fancy piano at a store that had gone out of business—his boss promised to buy it if it passed muster. He was ecstatic about this piano, but still he remembered to point to the key around my neck and gently shake a finger at me as he left. It was then that I thought I had to look. The closet was as important to him as his music, and perhaps more important than me.

Obviously, I couldn't stop myself. I tried. I called my mother's sister, Auntie Perfect, to try to get her to talk me out of it but she was in her car on a highway and yelled into the receiver "It's a bad connection, dear!" and hung up.

Soon, I was propelled down the narrow hall to the closet. My hands shook even though I knew Adam was far away. I opened the door, planning to quickly memorize the way the items were arranged so I could leave them the same. But things spilled out, tumbled down the hallway—a bracelet of shells, some painted coins, a peacock feather, a fan. I catalogued as fast as I could.

I got all the things that seemed to be skating across the buffed wooden floor and put them back, on top of photographs of Adam with his sister, and some with other girls, too. Holy trinity after holy trinity. Adam with Abby with a tropical tree, with his haircut from last year. Adam with a girl and car I never had seen. Adam with Abby beside a statue of a winged man. Adam and twins on a couch.

I wasn't surprised but I was sad. I didn't mind about the photographs, only that they were hidden—at the time, that seemed worse, though now I better understand. In any case I closed the closet door as quickly as I could, but every day until Adam got back, I reopened the door, sat on my knees until they were bruised and sore from the floor. I kept trying to arrange the photographs so he wouldn't know I had touched them. What if he had laid a hair across them, though? What if this was all a test?

But still I continued to look! And each time I opened the door, and even when it was shut, I saw Adam's other women. Eventually it became an obsession for me, like my love for him had once been.

Finally Adam was due home, very late on Saturday night. On the way to the airport to pick him up, I bought a spearmint facial mask at the store in a vain attempt to conceal my crime. I thought that covering my face could hide my guilt. Those masks leave only your eyes peering out like some wild beast's, and I felt that I looked strangely pretty in one of the masks, and natural.

I applied it in the car. "Green for your envy," I thought. "Green for inexperience. Green for rotten

137

love." My face was covered in a matte-lime color, like turned copper. The lines of the dried, cracked parts made me look like a near-shattered statue, and my eyes shone stubbornly behind. I drove intently forward, aware of a few odd looks glanced my way from cars going home from the taverns. Poor drunkards, I thought, being sober this time. I must have really scared them.

I knew Adam never suspected me of bad behavior but I could tell he was irritated with me when he got in the car at the airport's passenger zone. "What's on your face?" he said. "A mask?" I replied.

Still frightened of being found out, I kept the mask on even when we went to bed, so my face seemed heavy. I felt my lips weigh down. It was strange to kiss in a frown, and I don't think it pleased him. My face got heavier and heavier and finally he turned to the wall.

After that night I believe I began to push Adam slowly and methodically away. Yet at the same time, as sure as I was I would lose him, I tried to win him back. I grew my hair long, wore it pulled back off my face the way that he liked. Wearing thigh-highs on a regular basis, I arranged red bulbs in the bedroom lamps and kept fresh tulips on the tables. He always remarked on these aspects as if he were truly pleased. But over and over I'd falter again and ask him what was wrong. This displeased him more than anything. "Nothing's wrong with me," he'd say. "A better question would be what's wrong with *you*?" Then he'd shut himself up with his music.

After a bit I became pregnant, quite by surprise. The doctors were puzzled when, in the second month, I came down with chronic laryngitis. Adam stopped talking to me, to protect my voice and give me rest. Also, his silence would allow him to write some music before the baby came. He said it was good for him. "You don't really want this baby," I'd say. "Your laryngitis is a good thing," he'd answer, "because I won't want it if you keep talking."

I lost that baby after three months, just like the other, and I have to admit I still blame the other women. Not that it was their fault—not at all—or Adam's for having them. It was rather that I couldn't get them out of my head, so there was no room inside for anyone else, let alone me. I had became too thin in every way, too thin to carry a baby.

The most ridiculous thing was I continued to sneak a glance into that tiny closet every single day. I just wanted to see if Adam had taken a look—and sometimes the things would have shifted a little, and I knew that he had. Also, occasionally I would find something different, some new artifact of a girl. I didn't know where these came from or whether they were past or present. Light glinted off the photographs always spilling out luminescent.

It is strange that Adam's lies infuriated me when I too was lying, I guess, ferociously and often. I would imagine this all contributed to the later distance between us.

chapter thirty-five

The Gold girls sat in a line on the couch, waiting patiently for dinner. On the television three sisters in calico dresses played in a creek, their ma and pa close by in their house that was built inside of a hill. Soon Mrs Gold would deliver the girls' thawed-out suppers. For Merry, Salisbury steak, a flat oval of meat for a simple girl of simple taste. For Lucy, macaroni and cheese, which she always ate with a huge wooden spoon, being strange. And for Ketzia, hot turkey, because she liked the way its stuffing hid under a blanket of bird. Secret things always pleased her.

But when the food was placed before her, Ketzia only picked at the meal. Do you want to know why? She was already full from her first guitar lesson, held in a dark building made of stone, two miles from the Gold's home, the Académie Musicale. It was there Danilo taught and gave lessons to Ketzia for free. Mr Gold had arranged this with Danilo, his friend, over the summer in some kind of significant trade that involved golf. But the guitar was too difficult for Ketzia to master. She never managed at all! From the beginning it made her stomach hurt.

Imagine a small girl in a rumpled poncho hand-knit by her grandmother—in itchy red wool—

sitting in a dank hallway, guitar case beating against her knees in rhythm with tunes that streamed under a door. She waited there, breath held against the pending failure. "Isn't it good, Norwegian would..." Ketzia heard from inside the room. Would what, she wondered, would what, would what? It was one of the most beautiful and mysterious things she had heard in her life. Finally, it was her turn inside. But the unwieldy guitar—too large in her too-small hands, held by a left-handed girl taught by a right-handed man—proved an impossible instrument to learn.

That particular afternoon she had nearly fainted from fear when Danilo showed her a B minor chord, and asked her to play it herself. Placing the guitar quietly across her lap, she whispered merely, "I can't." And it wasn't a lie. Staring at the page of music, she tried and tried. But the notes, just as all the numbers in school, merely danced off the page and in front of her eyes in a taunting manner that made her cry. She ran her hands along the strings for him, making a terrible sound.

Danilo paced the room. "That is not very good," he said with a smile. "What do you propose I teach you instead?" She was supposed to learn to play and sing, sad songs she'd already selected. They had names like "Sunrise, Sunset" and "Life is a Cabaret!" So, despite dull fear that Mr and Mrs Gold would someday uncover the lie and ask her to play for them, together they devised a plan. Is it any wonder that even now, hearing a guitar still makes Ketzia ashamed, and that she will never, ever "sing" on command? She had years of practice at *that*, to be sure—with Danilo and starting at ten.

Returning to the night after that lesson and one of the first agreements made between her and a man, it is important to remark that, for Ketzia, this was the beginning of a long and unpleasant relationship with television programs about girls who lived on the prairie, and danced to their pa as he fiddled.

"The Beginning of a Long and Unpleasant
Relationship"

chapter thirty-six

Some True Miracles

Once there was a poor piano player whose wife made everything miserable for him in his home. The musician was Adam and the wife was me. He despised his employment, even though I reminded him how shoppers traveled just to hear him—not even to buy clothes. But even though I knew how upset he was about his work, I continued to make things worse.

One day he came home from work at midnight instead of six p.m. "Fun day at the mall?" I asked in a falsely bright tone. Then I methodically placed down his dinner and sat staring while he ate. I watched each bite from plate to mouth with exaggerated attention. Halfway through the food he got up and took some stale white bread from the pantry.

"What, now you don't like my cooking?" I said. Finally, he couldn't stand it anymore. "You're incredibly boring," Adam said. He threw the spaghetti in the dog's bowl. "What do you mean?" I answered. "And that's not garbage." Adam was already halfway down the hall. "And you're not, I suppose?" I added. "Boring, I mean, not garbage." I began pounding on his study door. "Please, let me in. I didn't mean to complain!" But *stupid Ketzia, stupid loon,* I muttered as well, though Adam hated when I called myself names. But those rhythms will come to your head if you don't watch out.

In order to counter this turn of events, I decided I'd make myself beautiful for him. In the bathroom I applied velvety shadow to the lids of my eyes, rose stain. Mascara I swiped on the lashes in thick strokes, several. I clamped the curler on a little extra. I glossed my lips again and again.

Standing over Adam's face as he lay in our bed, I tried to droop my eyes in a seductive yet foreboding pose. "I'm sleeping," Adam said. I turned on my favorite lamp: its base was the female form, its shade a desert sunset. Adam rolled over and groaned. "Don't worry, everything's fine." "Don't you want me to get in bed?" I asked, and heard a weary groan. "Won't you play me some music?" Silence. I left the room in the orange light.

Eventually, I fell asleep beside the couch on the cowhide rug—the animal smell very relaxing somehow. When I woke up, Adam had gone. Outside the house I turned off the front light, extinguishing all hope. "No light tonight," I said aloud glumly. "Not for Ketzia." I looked around for the dog to kiss but seeing her, I felt no kinship. I wanted—O how I wanted— and then, alas, I kicked at poor mutt, or at least at the air all around her. "Get away, get away from me, Doggerina," I started crying. And the stupid mutt just kept after me, her tail between her legs and her mouth open in a nervous grin.

"Okay, okay," I conceded. I locked the chain on the front door and reached down to pat her head, which was damp because she liked to stick it in the toilet. "Poor loser," I said. "You sure are mine." I poured a tumbler of vodka and some for the dog and found something to watch on television. On the screen a lot of people danced sexily, dressed. I joined in. What else could I do?

Staring at the blue light, into the bodies beyond me, I felt a wave of disgust. I had a strange awareness of how everything that once was light could eventually darken. This was too much for me to stand, because I had never expected good things, and now would lose them. Frantic, I sprinted from the room, dragged my feather boa from under the bed and danced with the dog. I put the boa on my shoulders like wings. I hopped over its ends like they do in some churches, with snakes. The dog tried to eat the pink feathers and I encouraged this bad behavior, as apology for before. I folded one knee like a wild flamingo and hopped.

After not very long I felt a chill wind on my back. I heard Adam's voice. "Ketzia, open up, it's freezing out." I muted the tube and walked to the door. Adam peered through the window at my goose-fleshed skin. When he came in smelling of gin, he patted the dog. "O Doggerina, what a *good* girl." "Now you love her more than me?" I said, as if I hadn't realized *how pathetic*.

But Adam never stayed mad at me long. I was lucky that way. He put on a jazz record and undressed, and then forgave me on the spot— well, on a spot several feet below. I was a little afraid but I let him. I guess I wasn't so boring after all.

The next morning when Adam woke up he simply said "Thank god for women." "Thank god for *gin*," I corrected. We let Doggerina get in the bed. "My two girls," Adam said. The three of us slept all the way until afternoon then, but it seemed like we slept forever.

chapter thirty-seven

What appears to be an increased social tolerance toward affairs has lately rendered business at Triple D slow. But perhaps it's just a lag, or the weather. People in every age are just as unhappy in love as the people of any age before. It's been raining a lot, which may serve to deter many trysts, I believe. Yet, even knowing this phase will end, I find myself at loose ends with time. The scant material detectives bring in is quickly dispensed with because of my speedy typing. And their dictation lacks fervor, and occasionally gets resentful: "Subject seems to be limping slightly. Who cares? The schmuck. Get a life." For the time being I've run out of work.

Most of the workday now the detectives have taken to sitting in the back office, telling dirty jokes. I hear them repeat one they especially like, about eating a "box lunch at the Y." I find myself getting bored by them, which is shocking. I have always valued my ability to entertain myself with whatever I find around me. When I was younger, counting my teeth with my tongue was alluring. Counting blades of grass. Counting birds. Yet even if the men invite me to join them, I decline. In any case I do have a big project now with those books to retype.

Typing is my career, after all, and not talking. There is, of course, some concern. I have heard I may be replaced some day by a voice-recognizing computer. So far the technology is unreliable, but I'm sure they'll master it soon. They always do, master these things.

Yet for now, even at home, I divert my attention from all verbal discourse. For example, whenever I absolutely must speak on the phone with my mother, I type the whole thing out on the table with the tips of my fingers. This keeps me in processing shape, and free of attachment to her, which I find somehow grueling.

Abstractly, of course, I really adore her. I adore everyone, if you want to look at it that way.

chapter thirty-eight

Ketzia and the Penitent

I must admit, even I, who criticize no one, was somewhat shocked when Adam told me what he had done. As much as I loved him, I found it quite strange. I knew he'd been frustrated with his career, despite his attempts to conceal his disappointment at being a department store entertainer. He had also started playing Sunday nights at a bar, an awful dive with peanut shells on the floor and only no-name cans of beer.

It started when the weather changed, soon after he started that gig. A western wind blew dead leaves on the roof and branches against the windows, closing me in; the gusts were so strong that I could hear them bang out tunes on Adam's piano when he was gone. Clouds twisted silently through the sky and a seemingly constant thunder made the air always grey. I tried walking to embrace the cold, and for some time I found the bite of wind alembic against my face and covered limbs. But over time the cycling sky came down on me fiercely.

Adam was gone much of the time, devoted to his music no matter the scene. He was in a bad mood because of the venues, but spent hours and hours working his way. This left me alone with tornados.

One day a cyclone tore off a piece of our house while I cowered in the cellar below. Among the roots, I hid with Doggerina, who howled. A storm started suddenly inside me as well. Poor little girl, I comforted her. Poor little sweetheart, down here below.

Afterwards, day and night you couldn't tear me from books or the dog. I wore my hair in a girlish tail, high on my head, and put a ribbon around Doggerina's neck. I read everything I'd read as a kid out loud to her. My favorite, which I tortured Adam by narrating time after time, was a book for eleven-or-so-year-olds, about some Jewish sisters living in a city. They ate soda crackers and lox. In my favorite chapter one of them racked up a huge overdue bill at the library. Adam didn't really see the appeal. He read books on music theory and time. He bought me two books he thought I'd like, one about a procedure for 'forcing flowers' indoors and one some sort of philosophy tract about a seducer. But I knew I wasn't as smart as that—nor was my pet. I stuck with the tales of those girls.

One day, curled up on the cowhide carpet all day beside Doggerina, with books in pastel colors and little, easy words, I devised a small plan.

It just came on. One moment I was reading, and the next, I was cleaning the cupboards and tossing out empties (spice shakers, cleansers, bottles of gin). Each time I found a bottle of pills I emptied its contents to the palm of my hand. Down my throat they fell in a thick parade. I wavered to the bedroom. Trembling with a bra, I chose a red, fuzzy coat and some jewelry—huge silver hoops, three puzzle rings, two tarnished charm bracelets (with a teakettle and scissors, ballerina and grapes). I pulled the hood because my head was quite cold. Later, I woke on top of the bed, my hair all messed up in a tangle.

"Spread like a book, you mean?" I asked Adam. He was telling the tale of how I lay there. "No," he began again, after too much coffee at an espresso bar. We had paid many dollars for tiny glasses of caffeine. "I've told you a lie, I'm sorry, Ketzia. Looking into the bedroom, I saw you on our zebra-sheets, wearing that animal jacket. I pictured you roaming the streets while I played. I was in an awful mood. I thought of your body inside." "Do you want me to put on that coat once we're home?" I asked with an edge. There were many teenagers at the espresso place and perhaps they had heard. Some of the girls had fluorescent hair, others, ink-black and dull.

"First," he continued, "I watched some basketball. That player you like with the sunburst tattoo? I felt like he was telling me how to be cool. I went back to you. I touched the mirrored wall with my head." This was a long story for Adam to tell.

"The whole time your fingers were still. When you're awake, they're always tugging at me. It didn't take long before that color of your hair drew me in, with that impossible brown-green, and I lifted the vinyl and then, easy as that, I came."

But I remember the scene a little bit differently, how I *did* move my arms, my bracelets dangling off them. My charms brushed his skin, their metal edges dug in. His back burned, and above, the bedroom light flared, then dimmed.

Later that year Adam's oldest friend visited from far, far away. Ivan is big and has long grey hair—he's really good-looking. Together we drank jars of moonshine, a new product from the liquor store. It was cornshine, really, tasting of poison. We sat on concrete blocks in the yard. "I'm so relieved you're better," Ivan turned to me, taking a swig. "Better?" I echoed. "What do you mean?" I took a swig too, resisting the urge to spit up. Then, I liked keeping up with the guys. Doggerina trotted away, repulsed by the smell.

"Okay, okay," Adam said that night in bed. Ivan had left, as quickly as he'd come. "I haven't told you the whole thing. While you were sleeping I noticed how your lips were deep red, I guess because you were thirsty. But they looked painted, I mean like a painting. After a while Ivan showed up from out of nowhere." Ivan's always doing that—appearing as from air, like an angel. "So I showed you to him. Obviously, I noticed how he was looking at you and I thought it'd be better not to tell you yet."

"Tell me what? That Ivan was over that time? Why?"

"Stop asking me why. 'Why' is never the question to ask. You always say you wish men would watch you more. I just let him look. Of course we were drunk. Later, I woke up in bed and saw your underwear twisted around my ankle, your bra on my wrist. Only then did I remember Ivan, and he was right there."

"And what did he say," I said, my face glowing hot. "He'd watched me with you. He said it looked like I was breathing life back into you, tenderly." I nodded slowly, warming back despite the original lie. "That's sweet," I said, almost crying. I had a very soft spot for Ivan. "Ivan's too metaphorical," Adam finished. "I just wanted to lie with you as my wife."

When we were first together I *knew* Adam was mine. The way I recall it, he'd tell me I was his Blackamoor Queen. He would say things like "Ketzia, you're my Indonesian Sky-Girl. Yeah." I don't even know what those things are. Once, he promised to bring me 'pink-skied mornings if time would allow,' and then, he said, morning would 'turn into a night sky of a hellion of colors and jewel-candy trees would open up into it.' Nothing fancy would be there, he said, except a cluster of houses and faint, almost unnoticeable birds in the stars.

On what occasions would he say these things? I can't remember. It just seemed he was always

157

saying them. Or maybe it was me. We drank a lot, I think. But you see I understand Adam. He was sky-rocketing. Birds always rested on his shoulder in my mind, spiraling up, which made him inhumanly good. I heard music in my ears even when I thought I was dead, and it was because of him I stayed alive, I believe. So I knew what he was thinking even if he didn't speak.

When he told me about Ivan and him, I said over and over that I was secretly pleased at the thing. I said, in fact, I had been quite aware at the time, which he pointed out meant there was no secret at all. "I don't see why," I'd answer. Then I always corrected myself—"I mean *how*," having learned about why.

But on further consideration I have to admit to myself—never him—that I don't remember anything about it at all, except maybe the precision with which I had pulled the fur hood on my head, then gotten in bed for what I thought would be days.

chapter thirty-nine

The Ditmarsh Tale of Lies

I'm going to tell you something. I saw two roast chickens flying, they flew swiftly with their breasts turned heavenward and their backs hellward. An anvil and a millstone swam across the Rhine, as slowly and quietly as you please, and a frog was sitting on the ice at Whitsuntide, eating a plowshare. Three young fellows on crutches and stilts were trying to catch a hare. The first was deaf, the second was blind, the third was dumb, and the fourth couldn't move his feet. Do you want to know what happened? The blind one saw the hare running across the fields, the dumb one shouted to the lame one, and the lame one caught the hare by the collar. Some men wanted to sail on dry land. They set their sails in the wind and sailed across great fields. In the end they sailed over a high mountain and were miserably drowned. A crab was chasing a hare, and high up on the roof lay a cow, who had gotten there by climbing. In that country the flies are as big as the goats in this country. Open the window and let the lies out.

chapter forty

Adam and the Girls

Often we went to bars in the evenings. There was little else to do where we lived. Once, sitting down and looking around, Adam would laugh and say "What luck I have to be with you, because I can be with other girls— one by one without wasting time—and you'll still be my Ketzia." Occasionally this made me laugh. I would be in a form-fitting sweater and skirt, and my hair would be parted just-so. Smoking a cigarette, I would lean my head to one side. "Do whatever you want," I often said with what—I hoped— appeared an indifferent sigh, such as an actress might do. I thought of one movie star in particular, a blonde whose husband had filmed her a lot in plots full of love and insanity.

But if I had too much whiskey before this exchange, I would begin to shake, and, retreating to the ladies' room would weep. I always became very depressed by grimy linoleum and mirrors. Applying my lipstick, I would hope Adam would just take me home, and not one of them. "Will it be me?" I'd say into the reflection. If in a particularly bad mood, "And who the hell are you?" I would answer. From time to time, returning to the table and recognizing my fear, Adam became unmoved, and said "I'm not going to be manipulated like that. You have to be more confident, Ketzia. This has nothing to do with us. We're *great*."

I understood that because I believed him. He had good ideas and a pretty good heart. We had a terrific time together, talking, drinking, doing nothing at all. Besides, I had also desired other men, which had no negative effect on him. My insecurities were not his problem. Could he help it if good-looking girls remained in the world, giving him desiring glances? And indeed, how was it his fault that, caring deeply for Adam, I occasionally encouraged him to leave bars with them?

One such night a young bartender poured him a flaming drink. Beside him sat a girl in designer jeans. She shoved her hand in a pocket and arched her back, leaning her head forward and looking past me at Adam. To my left, a girl I knew he'd been seeing stared pointedly in another direction. She was very young, and had once been a piano student of his. She wanted to learn only love songs, he'd said. I tried to clear my head. Sucking my beer fast through a straw, I ordered another and turned toward Adam.

"Hey you, Adam. If I have to live such a sordid life, at least let me ask you one thing." I was trying to be humorous. Adam sighed. "Ketzia," he said, "don't ruin the evening for me." "What's there to ruin?" I asked. "You don't want to go home with me, and I won't make you." Adam looked a little bit happy at that. He was really so easy to please. "Fine," he said. "What do you want?" But he looked at me with some trepidation, still.

"Well," I began. "How about, whenever you leave with another girl and I go home alone…" but I couldn't think of anything for which I might bargain. I lit a cigarette and considered my options. "I guess maybe I could get a job to keep me distracted," I said. "I think I would make a really good typist, in fact." Ordering another fiery concoction, Adam turned my way. "You're smarter than that," he said, with a genuine smile. Then he sipped his beverage contemplatively, relieved the trouble was done. This all hurt my feelings somehow.

The bartender lowered the lights and glanced at him from under her bangs. I raised my eyes. On the ceiling was a mythic scene—ghost-like gods painted on black, with fake vines and red bulbs woven into the rafters. I wished myself into it, closing my eyes. When I opened them I was still at the bar. I slid off my chair and patted Adam goodbye. "I'm going home to practice my typing," I said. "Have a nice night." He ordered another drink as I left.

When I got to our house—a mobile home, really—I pulled out three machines: my old electric typewriter, a pink plastic children's one I'd gotten at a thrift store, and Adam's portable computer. I put on a record of a family band, with a singer who'd died of starvation. She had a low, gorgeous voice and, against the poppy sound of the songs, it made music more tragic than most. I took a beer from the fridge and listened a bit, sitting on the couch with the dog.

After a while I began typing lyrics. I'd lined the machines up, and now moved among them. The first, electric, went too quickly. "Hanging around." The second, much slower, sounded sadder. "Nothing to do but frown." Then I moved on to the computer, with its silent stealth. It was just right. I kept typing this song over and over electronically, thinking Adam would come home and find me. For some reason I thought he would be very impressed. I felt somehow elegant, typing, and quite erotic. As if, when men saw me, they would see my essence and know how I felt, or see it reflected on the screen.

In fact, I felt completely myself standing there. I watched the whole performance in the night windows, thinking "Ah, I see." In a way it helped me understand how Adam felt when he looked at women, because often I felt the very same way— that is, when I was myself, looking at me. It's hard to explain, but I couldn't admit it unless I was typing, I think.

I wanted to share what I had figured out with Adam, but that night he stayed out a really long time, until morning, in fact. I had put all the machines in their cases when he finally returned, very tired.

"A Really Good Typist"

chapter forty-one

Standing in the Flying Fisherman, which was also Unit No. 3 at the Emerald Ocean Motel, young Ketzia breathed in deeply, ready for work. Always she had anticipated tasks with excitement. Despite fake wood paneling all around, there was a sticky scent of sap, thick in the muggy air. The motel owners let her clean cabins on Saturday mornings in exchange for a bucket of chowder from the motel café, on which the entire Gold family could feast. This had always been fun, a tradition of many years. Ketzia found pleasure in menial things.

She had felt from a very early age an affinity for chores, frequently enacting the scenes of drudgery of fairy tales and movies. Ketzia liked one movie in particular, where a rich little girl was abandoned by her father, forced into labor as a scullery maid and made to carry coals in a bucket to mean girls' rooms. But the movie took a sorely disappointing turn near its end when the father returned, the girl treated as a princess again.

That day she carried a bucket of supplies: lemon-scented wood polish, sea blue glass cleaner, powdered scrubbing solution. In the other rubber-gloved hand she clutched yesterday's newspaper;

newsprint doesn't leave streaks, it leaves no trace at all. She had the whole day free and could take her time to do this well. Mr Gold had taken the other kids to tennis, while Mrs Gold slept in. Ketzia liked the public tennis court well enough. It was lined with overgrown beach roses and had a cracked, neglected surface, but she liked it as one would like a secret garden, not as the location for "family fun."

Kneeling on the threadbare carpet of No. 3, she sprayed some polish on the coffee table, a piece of driftwood resting on a carved wooden seagull base. She patted the seagull's head. Next, she dusted every light bulb with care. After the mirrors, the bureaus, the kitchen counters and table, the windows in the attic space—with hot air like breath—and the shower that thundered when you touched it, the job was almost complete. However, the experience was far too brief. Emerald Ocean Motel employed what its manager called 'real girls' to do the 'real cleaning,' and Ketzia only came in to do touch-ups at the end.

This Saturday Danilo showed up to help her as he occasionally did. That, too, had quickly become a tradition when he had arranged his summer vacation around the Gold's, staying in the motel right beside them. As usual, finding Ketzia alone, he played on an unplugged electric guitar and sang what he called Scrubbing Tunes: "Dusting, Dusting," "Vacuuming Girl" and "Polish!" Next came pure instrumentals, to which Ketzia danced on a table and removed all her clothes with the moves of a stripper. At his request she left on the gloves. She found cleaning games far more dangerous than "Punish," and shook. Her hands sweated under the rubber.

She understood, of course, that if it were your destiny to be a maid, you were meant to be servile. Newsprint did leave marks on the knees, but Danilo helped her remove them. Afterwards, he agreed that she was well suited to chores and to choring. And he understood her better than anyone else, he said. She could trust him completely, more than even her parents.

"Danilo says I'd make a good maid," Ketzia murmured into her plate at the dinner table back at home, months and months after the summer. Perhaps Mr Gold was merely surprised because she'd been silent so long, but he replied in very harsh tones. "Don't be ridiculous, Ketzia, he said no such thing. He thinks someday you'll be a star," he said, though he hadn't even inquired how the lessons were going, or asked her to perform for him at home. "Oh," she replied, hanging her head. She tried not to cry, but Mr Gold saw. "Stop being so weird," he said, and left the room. Her sisters followed him, smirking.

Sitting in silence, Ketzia watched as Mrs Gold methodically emptied the table of dishes, slid on rubber gloves at the sink and tore into the cleaning.

chapter forty-two

Adam Brown and Ketzia Gold

The real end was trying. We had no idea where to begin. For days, out dull-eyed windows we stared at dull-brained neighbors who were always eating weeds with machines. At twilight we'd have sex in the yard and hope to lift the whole world and ourselves out of a stupor.

And we drank all the time, at all hours. A bachelor with eyes like coal had sold us this shell of a house, and when drunk, I found I had lurid thoughts about his life. "I feel that we're never alone," I'd say. I'd see his face in the windows, in the closets, the sink. I would become inconsolable, wanting him gone. Then, I would apologize to Adam for obsessing about him. But Adam criticized my 'sorries'—"They're insulting to me," he'd say, flinging bottles in the yard. Beer bottles, whiskey bottles, brown glass, green. They fell to the lawn and I'd feel serene. Adam was king to my stilted queen.

The other houses were so close I heard neighbors talking. The walls were thin and echoed. *Mirror, mirror on the wall, who's the whitest trash of all? Ketzia Gold and Adam Brown, girl and boy with dirty lawn.* I hid inside as often I could, but inside was difficult too as the bachelor lurked there, watching me all the time, especially when I was changing.

We had almost no money so had to design home entertainment. At night, watching lights come on was a short activity the city provided. There were three tiny skyscrapers that lit up the scene in a pattern with red and green lines. The unfolding of plastic chairs on the porch was itself quite an occasion. The trucks going by on the highway became a song. In this house we had dimmers and I'd play them, up and down, until Adam begged for mercy from the alternating darkness and light.

There were other distractions as well. One room had a ceiling in mirrors—a dirty reminder of that bachelor. And in another, instead of running water we had a beer tap, something I had never seen in a home.

Adam found things of his own to enjoy. Next door lived a beauty and I watched Adam watch her. That long-legged woman, how could I ever compete? Sometimes I saw her catch his glance and leave her door ajar. A sighting of her always forced me to early drink. That's where the story kind of begins.

I'd spy through the curtain as he left every morning. I knew what occurred but I wanted detail. Did he greet the girl next door on his way to his job? Did he hide in the bushes and sneak in

172

the back? Would she wear her beige suede pants or a skirt? O, these questions were far too difficult for me. So, simply as an experiment, I became quite the little crackerjack with our fine beer tap.

Tapstress, barmaid, old maid me.
Tho' I thought I had a husband
And the husband he had me.

Now, I'd say it takes exquisite skill to conjure a scene and dress for it as if it's real. In my strappy old heels and a short, short skirt, I learned to tell a hawk from a handsaw. Crook the old elbow, I'd say aloud, swilling a few.

Come summer I brooded like a vulture in the backyard all day until it was over, cigarette in hand, my soul smoking away. I would watch the evening sun fall behind trees. Campers lumbering by in bright yellow machines, something in my stomach rising to greet me. Hello, mad Ketzia, goodbye sweet day. All this, I can say with conviction, was never fun for Adam. "But *why* do you hate me," I'd cry. "Even though I know that I'm not beautiful." Other times I felt alive. "Don't hate me because I'm so beautiful," I'd flirt.

It was tiring, being drunk so often. I vowed I would make things nice for us again. I would make them nice not only as my mother had made them nice for my father but how I wanted them to be nice for me. I would make them real.

I began with a small idea, that bacon would make a surprising and fattening meal for Adam,

173

who in response to my sadness was wasting away. Shopping was light at this time of year, requiring much less piano, and he took long lunches away from the mall. It had been some time since I had prepared a good one for him. I put on old jeans, knotted a bandana into a halter, and tied my hair with a shoelace. I pulled on sandals and strapped an anklet on each foot. I checked myself out in the mirror, nodding at the man I saw alongside me. He nodded his approval and followed me to the kitchen, I think.

There, I started some bacon. As the strips began to warm, I happened to remember how well beer goes with it. "I'll pour one for him," I thought. "And one for myself as well." I thought one beer wouldn't matter—this was a special occasion, after all, a special meal, the start of things getting better. I went to the tap to draw a beer. *Remember the draught handle was a mermaid and silver? You held a bare gleaming breast when you used her.*

With one hand on my hip I thought of the bacon cooking, and remembered the dog, loose in the kitchen. There she was, outside the window—I bolted into the bright and was blind for a second. By the time I could steady and see, the dog was way across the lawn, long slices of bacon dangling from her mouth on both sides. Her eyes were wide open, ecstatic with fear. I ran after the dog ("No, Doggerina, no!") but she had reached the edge of the yard before I got to her, and dragged the bacon across the dirt. A truck carrying mirrors drove by and I shaded my eyes. I shook my head at the dog, who hung hers in shame.

Slowly, I walked back toward the house. I knew we had more bacon as I'd been hoarding it for days. As I neared the doorstep my flowers ached at me, faceless suns with stunted smiles. I dragged a serpentine hose on the ground and spattered water against my palm. Suddenly, I heard the telephone ring. I rested the hose on the lawn and ran. "Hello-o," I said, but no one answered, and just banged their own phone down. This happened all the time. Usually, I called Adam at work right after to ask him which girl it may have been, but this day I vowed good behavior.

I poured myself another beer. But as I clung to the mermaid's fish-scale waist, I saw water seeping in from a corner of the room—the trailer had no foundation, just sat on the ground. I raced outside again and saw I had drowned all the flowers. Doggerina squatted upon them and peed.

So, readying for Adam's arrival—which had to be smooth—I took the dog by her collar and tied her loosely with a rope to a tree. Sauntering inside, I hardened to the sound of poor Doggerina crying. That noise was common. "No, Doggerina," I said. "No."

When Adam loped in for lunch, he was pleased with the beer and bacon. "This is just like in an all-night bar!" he said. With long fingers he slaked hair off his forehead and eyed me over his glass—with a look that was neither friendly nor demeaning.

Later, when Adam was about to go back to work, I told him everything that had happened.

"It isn't as pretty as it looks," I said. "I'm lousy in bed and I don't tell the truth." Adam sighed. "Forget it," he said. I touched his arm gently. "Can I ask you to do something for me?" I implored. He agreed.

With Doggerina's rope, so loose on my wrists like feathers or weeds, he tied me to the bedposts. I twisted my feet into each other, imagining them like a bird's, and he tied them too so I couldn't move. I could hear the dog crying outside the door. "It's okay," I said aloud. But in my head I rhymed, something that often happened when I was unhinged. *Doggerina, Doggerina, singing by the bed, don't you know your Ketzia Gold is a dumb nuthead?*

Adam lowered his head down my body and his hair smelled like bacon and beer. I looked up at the ceiling for the bachelor, but he was hiding from me. I wondered if Adam thought of the girl next door just then.

chapter forty-three

My life is completely in order, I think. How lucky I feel to have managed the complexities of modern living. What makes it so different, so unusual? I don't know, exactly, but I do know that it helps to keep things simple.

Foremost, one must appreciate details. Myself, I choose to admire this little apartment, the way its light comes in through old-fashioned blinds. I like the streetcar rushing by at regular intervals, I cherish its sound. I find kindness in the way the coffee-shop men pour a morning to-go cup for me, and how they wrap my breakfast-roll up in foil along with a small pat of butter balanced on top. This butter itself I also find sweet: a tiny sliver sitting on a tiny cardboard square covered with a tiny piece of waxen paper. And I am pleased with the diary I keep, into which I have begun to paste pictures and mementos—including the paper from the butter on the rolls I daily eat.

Outside my home, I like many things too. For example the new keyboard my detectives have bought me. Built on a curve, it eases the wrists. I enjoy the graceful way I've learned to type, almost like a musician. I would take the art of transcription onto the street—if I were less of a coward at heart.

I could type what people said in my ear, I could type whatever they wanted! Things like, "I eat the overcurious," or "I have not come for peaceful purposes, but to fight." All kinds of secret things that only they and I would know.

Because, you see, keyboarding makes very little noise. That's part of why I like it so much. Only the most trained eye can make out words just watching the fingers land—thus, typing provides great privacy. Well, it is true that *I* can read keyboarding hands—just like the deaf can read mouths talking. But I have practiced transcription a very long time with unique devotion, and somehow I doubt others have discovered the passion.

Incidentally, this is a special skill which I have not revealed to this very day. And I think that's all I need to say, for it's a crock of butter for you, and a diamond for me.

chapter forty-four

A Topsy-Turvy Tale

Once upon a time in the country by the sea, four depressed girls were out walking and all of the girls were me. One of them wore glasses, one walked funny, one was undressed and the last never talked.

Eventually, the four-eyed girl saw a field loaded with flowers at the end of a cobblestone path. She said to the meek one, "Tell old swivel-hips to get us some weeds." The limping girl, who had scoliosis, wavered into the grass and got the thorn branches. She gave them to the naked girl, who wove a rose garland for the top of her head.

The bespectacled one led us all on. Squinting ahead, she saw what she saw and stopped in her tracks. She just couldn't believe her lazy eyes: a neon-lit bar, so crowded it was deserted. She went up to the bartender and, lifting her patch, said, "Please, four one-dollar beers." He answered, "It's three dollars a margarita," and gave them martinis with twists.

As they left sucking olives, they passed a man selling peanuts, but all their shells were empty. The skin-barer bought a bag of the nuts for the shy one, who thanked her with a nod of the head. The girl with glasses rolled her eyes. We all balanced peanuts on top of our heads and kept walking, thoughtfully chewing.

"All right," the mute one finally said, her mouth full of flowers. "I'll take care of things if you promise not to say I am dumb." That quiet girl was famous for starving them all. So they got her a tiny chicken, which she diced into giant portions, while the bad-backed girl danced to a.m. radio and the flirt made bedroom eyes. When no one was looking, the bespectacled girl took the chicken's head out of the garbage, wrapped it in paper and climbed onto the stove.

All the while the quiet girl was removing the limbs from that bird. When she finally succeeded her mouth opened wide, because its spindly feet landed right on her own and its wings attached to her back—without a word she flew out of the room. We got more and more hungry waiting around, but that girl never returned.

chapter forty-five

The Bad Wife

In the end I was not a good wife for Adam. I was faithful, pretty and mostly kind, but somehow this did not add up. My muddle-brain tried, of course, the whole time.

If Adam was sullen and locked himself up with his music, I would make a meal and set it out nicely. Early on there was an exchange involving macaroni and cheese and frozen fake sausage.

"Knock-knock," I said at Adam's studio door. "Sorry to interrupt. Dinner is ready when you are." I went into the kitchen, poured a large glass of wine and tidied up. Adam came out five minutes later, sat at the table, spread open a grey napkin on his lap, much like the span of a vulture's wing, and served us both some food. "You didn't have to cook dinner," he said. "I wasn't going to play very long, but could have grabbed something later." "I know," I answered. "I wanted to." I shrugged.

"This is delicious, Ketzia," Adam said, spooning some more to his plate. He meant it even though he preferred the real kind of meat. I never had to be afraid he would praise me when he did not like something because then, as with the home-made fish balls (made from pike and salted onions in an iron grinder), Adam would push the food around with a utensil and say, "I don't know about fish balls," a tiny pout in his voice, and I'd make him a can of soup instead.

All along Adam would say "This is delicious, Ketzia," and mean it. I made grilled cheese sandwiches and put surprises in their middles, between slices of bright orange cheese, such as sweet pickles and black olives. Those sandwiches I cut in triangles and lay a pile of chips between. I made noodles with sauces I conjured up in my head. "You didn't have to go to all this trouble," Adam would say. "We have frozen food." But I could tell he was pleased. "The noodles were excellent," he'd say, and take his plate to the sink. "A delight," I would agree, following him.

I made all kinds of exotic suppers. Once I made hot dog casserole like my mother's, a combination of grilled wieners and ketchup baked to golden perfection, and Adam said it was very good. I wiped a smudge of baked bean from my chin. Adam told me I looked sweet doing things like that.

Somehow, though, I strayed, stopped being so good. Adam often came home from work complaining of fatigue. "I'm tired like a bat," he'd moan. "Tired like a hedgehog." His fingers would droop from hours of playing. For days he'd seem distracted and would lie down with his brown scuffed shoes still on his large feet, his hands too weak to untie them, he said. "Song after song after song after song," he moaned. "Do people need live piano for shopping? I should have taken up banking." I soothed him, reminding him of his love for music, how it kept him alive. He'd turn to the wall, depressed.

But I couldn't leave him alone. "Do you want a snack?" I'd ask. "No," he would answer. I would interrupt him again and again. Finally, as I softly shut the bedroom door for the twentieth time, "Maybe," I'd hear, and happy to do something for my husband, tired like a bat, I'd go to the kitchen and open the fridge, let the soft glow of its automatic light illuminate me. I lined up my tools: a stick of butter, a knife, two pieces of bread and a package of cheese, black olives in a can.

"Sorry to wake you," I'd say a moment later, and peer into a darkened room. Adam's eyes were always already open.

We began to eat our meals in silence.

It wasn't long before I started doing everything backwards. "Do you want some potatoes?" I'd ask. All the same old questions. "I got some at the market, on special this week. If I put them in the oven now you can do chords for a whole other hour." "I don't know," Adam answered. "Maybe. On second thought, no. I'm really not hungry." So, I'd go make the potatoes, one for him and one for myself. I didn't even like potatoes—I found them too sad to eat, maybe because I'd been told they had eyes.

185

In any case I heard maybe as yes, no as yes, and yes—Adam's increasingly infrequent yes—as most definitely not. When Adam would say yes to something I would invariably talk him out of it, say "No, we don't have to." But if he said no, I just went ahead and did it. My ears were turning inside out, like Doggerina's did in wind.

As Adam left for work each morning he would make suggestions about what I could that day. This was good because I made many lists of things to do but had trouble organizing them. "Could you do a load of whites," he asked one time. "Only if you have a chance, I mean. I'm fresh out of socks." He gently kissed my forehead goodbye.

A load of laundry whites! I thought. Laundry whites! That's exactly right, I thought. Perfect.

Somehow though the day got filled with other things. I watched television talk shows (with themes like "My Mother She Slew Me, My Father He Ate Me") and ate vast amounts of oatmeal. I scrubbed the bathroom floor with an old toothbrush of mine. I even read forty pages of the telephone book, looking for unusual names. By the time I was re-arranging my closet according to color (browns together, reds together, pinks all in a row) and remembered about the white pile of laundry at the foot of the stairs, it was too late. White towels, white tube socks, white underpants, a white tuxedo shirt for work. I heard Adam come in the front door as I stuffed the clothes in the washer, and poured a generous stream of orange detergent onto it.

"Hey wait, can I grab a pair of socks," Adam said, behind me. "I thought I'd go for a walk." I turned to see him standing there naked. Adam never went walking, because his piano playing was so passionate, it was physically grueling. So this took me by surprise, and I burst into tears. "It's too late," I cried, watching water steam onto the clothes. "It's much, much, much too late." I turned my face up to his. "It doesn't matter, Ketzia," Adam said, a bright lilt to his voice. His gaze seemed to fall somewhere above my head.

He went for a walk in his old sneakers with no socks and it really hurt his feet. I touched them with a finger as he sat at the end of the bed that night. "Ouch," I said. "I'm sorry." "It doesn't matter," Adam said. "It's not important. I walked all the way down to the river, you know."

"Don't bother vacuuming," he said one morning. "I'll do it when I get home." While he was at work, I vacuumed.

"Leave the dishes, Ketzia," another day. "You always do them before I have a chance." So I did the dishes, even some extras like servers we never used.

If Adam did something nice, such as cook dinner for us, I'd eat until I was so full I'd have to go get sick in the backyard, not making a sound. He cooked pots of food I never thought to cook myself, simple foods in great abundance. I'd eat and eat and say "How good!" but I was a bad and secret wife, and this became even worse.

For not only did I disobey but I also began to apologize for everything. If Adam wanted to stay up at night drinking tequila, pass it back and forth like we used to, my eyes would droop before the moon even rose. "Sorry," I'd say, on the verge of tears. "I just can't stay awake." I'd go in the bedroom and leave the door open. Light would stream in from the living room where Adam drank alone, calling old friends on the telephone.

"Why did you leave the bedroom door open?" Adam always said, incredulous the next morning. "If you're tired you should just go to sleep! It doesn't matter!" I shrugged. "I can't," I said.

If Adam wanted to go to bed early—"I'm tired like an ancient moose," he might say—I'd put a record on and dance around the living room in a pink satin slip, running over to the light switch every once in while and dimming the overhead up and down to the beat of the music. "I'm sorry, Adam," I'd say at the bedroom door, which I'd open. "I can't sleep—I'm just not tired at all for once." Adam would gently shut the door on my antics. I didn't *want* to bother him!

Soon, Adam began to take long walks without me, along the riverbank. He found a place he liked to go, beneath a concrete bridge where the underside of the bridge was arches all in a row, like in a painting he'd shown me one time in a museum. I often asked to go along, but he said no. "There are berries there," he said. "They're choke berries, the red kind that is poisonous." He knew I had a bad habit of eating things that grew by the road, just to see what would happen. I believe this was not why he was not taking me, but only a secondary detail.

Finally he invited me along. This was on an afternoon I had already done three loads of laundry, and stood at the end of the bed pinning pairs of socks together with slightly trembling hands. I'd hardly eaten for days.

"I'm going out," he said, but left the front door ajar, which I understood meant that I could follow. I could tell by the way Adam held his head—stiffly, without looking around—that he knew I was close behind. As he approached the edge of the river I stayed ten paces back. This always bothered him, but my feet would not speed up. O I was bad. Adam stood under the bridge. I stood nearby.

"If you tried to reach the vanishing point," he said loud enough to for me to hear, "you'd probably come out on the other side of time." I stood in silent agreement. Adam turned and headed home. He looked at me for a long time, over his shoulder, as he walked. I cast my eyes along the brown, silty river, slowly pushing west, and then under the bridge, toward the far bank. Because of a drought it was quite thin, more of a stream than a river. I saw an image of bad Ketzia at every arch, she stood beneath each concrete arch in a smaller and smaller version of myself who stood and stared right back. I nearly disappeared. I left my selves at the river and walked home. I carried some berries in my hand gently—so as not to break their fragile skin.

As I sat quietly on the back porch while Adam cooked dinner, I watched the night sky become heavy-lidded, dark blue, and listened through the wind for the palaver of bad wives, all the tiny Ketzias trapped at the edge of a stream, calling my name. Adam called me in, and I stood slowly.

An egg, scrambled and cooked flat like a pancake, then rolled around a thin spread of jam—my favorite meal—Adam placed before me on a china plate. I ate in silence and let Adam put me in bed. He shut the bedroom light off and shut the bedroom door. "Go to sleep," he said. "My baby." And then I listened as he did the dishes.

What a tidy room this is, I thought. It is large and clean, the bed is wide. I had a real moment of clarity.

But the only words I could think of later, when Adam got in bed beside me, were "I'm sorry." But these were the wrong words, completely, I think. Then the night closed in upon me. I heard insects scream outside and it seemed they were inside my head and then they went quiet and everything was blank. I wanted to speak of beauty, of what I had seen so sadly. "I *am* a bad wife," I said out loud. "It doesn't matter, Ketzia," Adam said after a long silence. "Try to go to sleep." I didn't know if he meant it didn't matter that I was bad, or that I was not bad and should not worry. There was no chance I was going to sleep.

I sat on the front stoop all night listening to cicadas sing.

The next day I let Adam take me to the car and drive me to a doctor, a tall man who folded himself like a praying mantis into an enormous leather chair. He asked me questions to which I had no answers. Adam sat outside the room and read bikini magazines, a strange selection for a waiting room, we agreed later. "See?" Adam said. "You haven't lost your sense of humor." He was always so nice to me.

The doctor sent us right from the appointment to a pharmacy down the block, a long shotgun room with wooden floors and ceiling fans. There a nice, round man in a white jacket smiled. He gave me pink pills the size of hummingbird eggs to take in the lambent night.

Adam always poured chilled glasses of water to help me swallow them down. And sometimes he would sleep with a hand on my stomach, waiting for the bird to hatch. "I can hear its wings!" he'd say.

Yet those pills merely piled up in my stomach with fast-beating hearts of birds. Then, the fluttering spread from there to my hands. After a while I began to hope my soul would finally bloom. But I'd stopped taking the pink things by then. They didn't do much to help, in the end. They were certainly pretty, though. Pretty to think of and swallow. I stuck around as long as I could.

For a long time after, far and wide Adam was known to have retrieved his difficult wife from the bottomless pit of supplication. And later, when we were apart, I would go and sit at the edge of the river under the bridge, stare fixedly at the farthest arch, and think in wonder of his kindness.

THE END

Illustration Credits

p. 35 Photo courtesy of Sandi Brougham and Bill and
       Sarah Madsen Hardy.

p. 57 Poem from *Flower Children: The Little Cousins
       of the Field and Garden* by Elizabeth Gordon,
       along with drawing by M. T. Ross, courtesy of
       Random House, Inc.

p. 97 "A Lovely Half-Dressed Girl" courtesy of Liz
       Brown (photographer), Nadine Steklenski (styl-
       ist) and Karin Stack (illustrator).

p. 117 Image from *Chimney Corner Fairy Tales*, by
       Veronica S. Hutchinson, with illustrations by
       Lois Lenski, published by E. M. Hale and Com-
       pany, Eau Claire, Wisconsin, 1926.

p. 145 Little Red Riding Hood, c. 1862 (oil on canvas)
       by Gustave Dore (1832-83) appearing courtesy
       of the National Gallery of Victoria, Melbourne,
       Australia/Bridgeman Art Library; gift of Mrs.
       S. Horne.

p. 165 Illustration modified from an original image
       courtesy of Peter Arnell.

p. 181 Photo appearing courtesy of Roz Bernheimer
       and Deborah Harris.

Additional thanks to Brenda L. Mills at FC2, and to
Sarah Madsen Hardy, Susan Ramer and Lydia Millet.